Outline of My Lover

Outline of My Lover

Douglas A. Martin

Nightboat Books
New York

Outline of My Lover was originally published by Soft Skull Press in 2000.

ISBN: 978-1-64362-023-7

Cover design by Brian Hochberger
Cover art by Nick Mauss, *Untitled*, aluminium leaf and acrylic on panel,
     2014, courtesy the artist and Campoli Presti Gallery
Design and typesetting by HR Hegnauer
Text set in Sabon and Helvetica Neue

Cataloging-in-publication data is available from the Library of Congress

Nightboat Books
New York
www.nightboat.org

Foreword

by Hugh Ryan

In the late 1990s and early 2000s, a queer handful of books took on a central place among my friends, as well as the people I was not friends with yet but might someday be. We stuffed the back pockets of our oversized JNCO jeans with beat up paperbacks, flagging Michelle Tea top or Baudelaire bottom. We treated them somewhere between sacred text, samizdat, and shibboleth. They were the path and the sign you were on it. We were all two-shoes-too-goody to live life like our semi-fictional anti-heroes, but back then, just being a dyke or a fag was enough to make us feel like dissipated outsiders, even as we followed (most of) the rules.

Outline of My Lover was the last of those books, and the most affecting. A slim white paperback with sensually curved corners, it defied convention and category—was it non-fiction published as fiction that read like poetry? Or fiction that drew on non-fiction for its content and poetry for its form? It was genre-queer before we knew the term, and the undeniable physical fact of its uncategorizable existence was (to us) permission in material form: write well, and you could write anything.

Plus, it came with a lore: it was published by Soft Skull Press, an indie house in New York City whose first books were secreted together in the back of an all-night Kinko's copy shop. It was what our college 'zines dreamed of being in their next lives.

i

But it was the prose that really caught me—the broken rhythms and strange juxtapositions that gave *Outline of My Lover* its fierce intentionality. Every word felt not so much written as pinpointed on the page, measured as much as a unit of sound and space as a conveyor of information. Sentences adhered oddly, their stuttering syllables and profligate commas herky-jerky and extraordinary. Because I could not predict their wend, the lines demanded my fullest attention.

My inability to sleep in a strange bed with the boy across from me wakes me in the middle of the night. Down two flights of floors, our room on the second. Out the heavy metal door I go into roaming over the different dark of campus.

I walk waiting. Something is going to, something is going to happen to me.

Douglas's sentences made me breath in his narrator's time. Two people synced through something intangible—isn't that the essence of storytelling?

Outline of My Lover was a treatise on limerence, obsessive desire for something you can't have, at least not the way you want. Even in achieving a relationship with his guide star, the unnamed narrator knows nothing will last. His was a rarely articulated position: the cunning pathétique, whose acts of submission are as calculated as they are genuine. He gets what he wants by becoming what is wanted.

I am dying for him, in a sense, abandoning childhood and entering it at the same time, a new one, everything over to him and his hands to learn over, start under, again with my idea of who I am.

As queer twenty-nothings, this was a deliverance my friends and I longed for. We played regularly at reinvention, constantly finding new selves we thought might be ours. After *Outline of My Lover*, we read *The Haiku Year*—a book of poems collectively co-authored by Douglas and friends—and embarked on our own ambitious plan for a year of daily shared poems. Do I even have to tell you, we lasted a week?

Surprising ourselves only, we grew up (or at least older) and lost touch. *Outline of My Lover*, however, stayed constant. It was time condensed down into space, a piece of my history I could lend out—until the day it didn't come back. Occasionally, thereafter, I reached for it, like a tongue worrying the spot a tooth had once occupied, but it was gone, as completely and suddenly as my twenties themselves.

Or so I thought until I started writing. Seriously writing, not that piddly shit I'd been talking about doing for years. I'd find myself contemplating a banal sentence and wondering how I could break it to feel new again. I'd find myself contemplating the truth and wondering the same thing. In graduate school, I studied "nonfiction" that erased the line between genres, a skinny family tree's worth of books whose roots—or me—always reached back to that white paperback with curved corners. I'd internalized something from *Outline of My Lover*, less a lesson than a sensibility, or maybe a hunger. From a permission it had become a goad: write well, or why write anything?

When Douglas invited me to be part of the this anniversary edition, it felt like coming full spiral—returning to something I knew well, but on a new level. Again and again, his book has kissed up against my life and retreated, offering something new each time. Already, I look forward to our next encounter.

Outline of My Lover

for those who've helped in various moves

*...I am disappearing, he thought
but the photographs were worth it.*

Anne Carson, *Autobiography of Red*

I.

A) Let Hover

We're taken to a place with no roots. The house was red brick, divided into one, two, three living quarters. Across the street is an abandoned building. I am already a morbid child and wish it were a mausoleum, a place for me to sleep, among rich ancestry and traditions that glow particularly romantic. There are some concrete sewer pipes. When we are trying to be a family with the new man, my mother's new husband, we will go for rides down any and all streets we can find, looking at houses decorated inside and out with Christmas lights. It is too expensive for the electricity to do our own house. This is how we are together. My sister and I in the back seat trying to stay warm. When we weren't in the house, there would be a possibility for magic, something new. We would sit quietly in the back seat, looking at the lights. Lights like stars, but closer.

This was the season for change, time you could not sleep for your excitement towards some unknown promise, coming in life. One more day, more morning. One more exaltation to last through.

One morning you would wake up and it would be there.

Always as a child, I started pretending. I was pretending I was a girl. I was acting. I was a girl. I pretended I could have what I wanted. That I could change the world with just my wishes, just like that.

Soon as I grew up I wanted other things. I started pretending like I could have those too, like I knew no better.

If I jump out of the trees, I will fly. I think. I don't know why I think this. Or know this, know I feel like nothing else I see on earth. Not yet. I harbor myself up there in the big magnolia tree.

Boys climb trees so maybe I still am one. Maybe there is hope and a chance for me, still. Maybe. If I sit in the tree long enough. I'm not allowed to have pets because of my breathing, how I can barely. No dogs, no cats. Their furs aggravate my condition. I want something that is mine to care for, any kind of pet whatsoever.

At first I pretend the birds are my pets. They belong so completely to me I don't even have to keep them in cages. They roam free to the universe, and I love them so well, they always return to me.

My mother leaves my sister in the crib to take me to the playground, push me on the swing. It's right outside the back door, when we still live in the North, close to my mom's parents.

A time before I can remember, which only comes down to me through stories.

I don't want to play with the other boys. The pigskin became a sign of dad's drunkenness which led to fights, which come to conclude our family.

I'm still very small, still share a room with my sister. We are told to play with the other kids next door, the boys who have a father and want to be Superman. I make excuses why I should want to be someone else. Somebody has to be the girl, I say. There has to be at least one.

I am used to playing with my sister, my sister who lets me pretend I'm like her, a girl, so I'm not the only one like me in our family. I want the boys shut out of the system of my universe, because you can't keep them there. They're always flying off. But you can't escape them.

Meanwhile, my sister and I fight over which of us gets to be what girl on what TV show.

My sister will never have to try to be as smart as me. She was born with the higher IQ. Her genius is recognized. All through school when she gets to join the few smarter children for private lessons. We are attracted to the same brother down the street, but she's allowed to want to marry him. She's allowed to want what she wants, to go after it and get it, be secure in that knowledge.

My sister's friends become my friends. My mother's friends become the women I hear talk, voice concerns, sit around the table with at dinner time while the men sit in front of the television, watch sports, drinking like my father. Television blares.

My mother never truly believes in our young passions. Either that or she has what she feels are our best interests at heart. Particularly, I speak of an adolescent desire for fame. I always wanted to be known, for someone to know I exist.

My mother asks me if I know how many people want to be what I want to be. Do you know how many people can be? I will try all the avenues, exhausting them. I work on my body, work on my dancing, try to teach myself to be anything. I will even settle for the background a stage.

Acting, I memorize dramatic monologues.

Or I start writing books in the third grade, start, stop, full of characters I try constantly to be.

Anything to forget where I've come from, coming from where I do, that I might belong forgotten soon.

I always imagined my father with black hair. My mother, my sister and I are all blonde, so blonde it's white as children, and that's where I'm left, who I'm left with so must be where I belong.

That's where I go, with the women. With the fair-haired ones, the women I learn to talk like, first thing. Divided along those easy lines of distinguishing characteristics. When they divided their mutual possessions from the marriage, my mother got the kids.

I don't know how long it was before my father left my mother that he returned to his parents. Remarried, had more children, worked on cars, worked so hard he had to unwind, never had time to write.

The boy I was never gets a birthday card or a card for Christmas. Nothing from his father, no contact.

Father from the North, who moved us South. The father the boy will do nothing to ever continue the line of.

Third grade, history. They are telling us all in the classroom to hate England even though that's where we come from. We're nothing like that monarchy, the mother country. The teacher lists all the reasons for disdain we should memorize. I run home to mother and think I'm smart, so smart, and my mother who spent girlhood in England once saw the queen wave, along with the beauty of romance, told me all about the excitement she felt. She watched from the bridge, a road, how alive she felt, how beautiful this tradition was. How beautiful it could be.

I never forget that perspective my mother gives me, my own evaluation in the face of what I'm being told. An unaccepting mind grows restless. My mother makes me doubt school a long time ago, so I go back and begin to question everything, all my teachers.

We are left alone to fend for ourselves, my mother and her kids. No man in your house, even though I'm told by so many people that's what I have to be now. It was better for everyone involved including us kids that they separated and my father left.

There are men everywhere. We see that, my sister and I. But none are ours. We don't belong to anything surrounding us it feels like at times. The Church, town, school system.

The church has asked us to leave if my mother is going to divorce, to get away from the man whose fists come raining down.

At school we are the kids we play with who can swallow our entire lives, trash. I forget how to breathe. I tell my sister time and again that I am dying, repeat it until she calls our mother where she goes to work at the hospital during the day, leaving us so she can afford to feed us.

I need to be taken there.

I can never forget the feeling of my childhood and the hospital I lived in once. The nuns from the Catholic Church come to see me because already I'm close to death. I lie there with lungs breath is a struggle for, to even perform the function they're made for.

With rosaries, they come. Plastic blue beads and jade, mother of pearl, white diamonds.

The oxygen tent is clear plastic I lie under and look out at the world through. They come in habits, a procession of them to tell me, inform me, they are praying for me. They whisper, praying over me, while I'm inside of the tent and the oxygen is hissing into the air I'm sucking into wet lungs.

My school assignments are brought to me.

You, little boy, why don't you bring your mother back to the fold, Church. Your mother has gone astray, is, you must be strong, for her. You are. Convince her of your right, you have every right to hear the word of God. To come to church, to go to Heaven when you die. You are still Catholic, even if your mother no longer is, is excommunicated, you were baptized. Your mother is not dong right by you kids. You have a right to the love of God, she should not keep you from Church. You need the Church. The Church is your family. You need God's love in a time like this, his word, no matter how wrong your mother is, has been, when you're this close to death. You need to convince your mother to bring you kids back to church. You can sit in the back pew, it's all right for her to come as long as she doesn't consummate her new marriage with the new man. Then they will allow it. They will honor the new marriage, second, only abide it, if his body is never taken into hers.

The hiss of the machine that oxygenates my blood. I am just a boy, a virgin.

I am under the oxygen tent.

I can't go camping because of pollen in trees, and the wet leaves. Because of dampness, my lungs fill with a double pneumonia and chicken pox. Imagine how sickly I must look. I can't play sports because I can't run, you'll get out of breath, at least that's the excuse I use so often once I have been given it, who knows if it's still true. Do. I can't breathe, live. Can't last, I have no stamina, endure sickly, can't breathe.

I can't come out from under the oxygen tent because I have to be under where air is regulated, cool and moist on my skin.

School books are brought to me under there, the oxygen tent. I want no cross words, only books. The pumping machine allows me breath. I remain quiet there, quietly. Breathing. My mother has started to love a new man. My hands fold in my lap. Months. Every now and then I pray but I don't know to who. Vapor is created, a stillness. Still....

So aware of no taxing on my lungs, my heart, it's hard to breathe. It hurts when I breathe.

The vapor cool, no heat.

I am eight, I am eighty.

I can't breathe like my grandmother. I'm afraid I will die at this age, so young. I know I could easily die because I often can't breathe, how hard for me, but I can't cease, breathing, the machine brought in to breathe for me does. I am plugged up to it and it makes sure I keep taking air in.

My lungs, my heart, beating.

My mother tries to teach us pride. We may be poor, but we were always clean and nicely dressed. Or you kids were always fed.

You never wanted for anything. Early on I learned about the world.

Black is bad, or that's what my place tries to teach me, where I try to grow up but grow so skinny knees wobble. I break an arm three times, separate times.

Jumping out of that magnolia tree, jumping out of a swing, jumping off the roof of the house.

Jumping.

The next time your arm might not heal, the doctor tells me. My mother warns me.

I have her hair, so my father's must be black, bad, darker, harder to see certain times.

We go through three houses as I am growing up. All of those houses are rented, all moves to rooms never fully mine, never furnished without my mother's influence.

Even the bedrooms, the toys, the clothes, the sheets.

When my sister and I eventually go off to where we can, with money they will save from not having to pay to raise us now, my mother and her husband will buy a house for themselves.

The last house I know is right down the street from the one before it, in short walking distance. Less of a yard, no trees in the front, only one in back. So why do we go there?

Because it's a nicer house, even if it is smaller. And it always looks good to move.

We run through the sprinkler, my sister and I, sitting on the hot porch until we dry off. Then we can come into the house. My mother doesn't want us tracking our wet feet through. There's carpet in every room of the new house. Except my room and the kitchen.

When we have kids over to play, my mother prefers they stay outside. Play in the front or back yard. We see across the street the neighbors have a swimming pool. A big, white house, even though we think they are poorer than us. We wonder how they got all that. Disability payments, we finally figure out.

We walk through the woods behind the house we lived in before moving again, this place that was starting to feel like home. We have to go now. We walk through the woods to another neighborhood, other streets with large families.

When we bring some of them kids over, just once, poorer even than us, they see the huge bookshelf in our living room, an enormous set of encyclopedias. Mainly because of this, they think we are rich. They've only ever seen books in the school library.

This was when we still lived in that house with trees in the front yard, that house.

The trees so old their roots showed, came up from underground. Pine trees. We would play among them in the front yard among buckles and crevices, the gnarls, poking up among brown straw mats, no longer green, crisp with the sap gone.

I remember the day we were sold the encyclopedias. I'll never forget. Then we were still living in the first house, the smallest apartment. That's where we knew our father, the whole reason we came to this state. There he just left us.

My mother isn't remarried. A traveling salesman convinces her these books will be good for the kids, that we'll need them in school one day, they'll save us time, help us go to college. She won't have to find the time to take us to the library anymore. We'll have the advantage over all the other kids now. We'll be smart, have an edge. You do want your kids to be smart, don't you?

We'll make her proud. Just wait and see.

She cooks supper, once she comes home from work, has been working all day. This is before my sister and I want to stop eating with her when we get older, ask her to just stop cooking for us. We no longer want to eat that.

During summers, when we are out of school she makes us take over cleaning the house.

When we were younger, we would all clean the house together, the three of us. My mom, my sister, me. We would dust the shelves for the encyclopedias, the bookcase that came free with them. My mother plays the only Tammy Wynette album we had, D-I-V-O-R-C-E. It becomes our favorite, the only country we like. I don't understand how something so close to home soothes, but it does.

In the absence of family, my mother has us children. Sister and brother, son and a daughter. Alike, so close we look like twins.

All three of us. Everyone thinks so. Our family with two kids and one mother. Mother young enough, looks young enough to be our sister. Men at the grocery store tell her so all the time, when they're bagging our groceries. It's almost like we have no mother.

Only a friend, another sister.

And then one day, a stepfather.

My stepfather has a special love for my sister.

Af first, my sister is more normal, the more normal one of us two. She certainly seems a lot more well adjusted than me, makes friends easily. She hasn't shown my stepfather yet how completely outside of everything we can all be. He wants to force us to go play outside, tells us to get outside, for me to get my nose out of that book when I want to sit on my bed and read all day long, a book a day, forget about the neighborhood we live in.

The boy who sits behind me in homeroom in seventh grade I never talk to. He hangs himself one night, playing a joke on his parents. His mother found him.

We left you alone, my mother reiterates, left you alone to do as you pleased, whatever you wanted.

Because I read, start to learn for myself, how to go away one day, I stop learning to talk. Everything becomes imbued with so much more weight. I grow silent and numb. I think about how everything sounds. I only want words I know running through my mind, words I can control, easily understand. If I surround myself with enough they will not go away from me. I want the words to keep running through my mind.

They, the parents, would like for my sister and I to help more. The yards are always a source of contention. But we don't care about the yard. We don't want to go out there and look at where we live.

We could at least help my stepfather in the garden he is growing. We sure help eat the food. Every year he has a garden, every summer. Summers I hate.

He goes there to get out of the house, think. I stay in my room and wait for the days to end so I can go back to school.

He'll pay us to rake the yard, my stepfather says. Or wash one of the two cars we have now. Fifty dollars if I help him put brake pads on a car, a little side project he has one weekend. It's a valuable skill to learn, he says.

Just like my real father, he's a mechanic, too.

There are fights. They start again.

At first it doesn't even involve us kids. Who knows what is whispered, what behavior is objected to, what leads to the discussed desire for separation, shouted. Get out, get out.

Return to the same starting point.

You either continue together or you don't. You remain man and woman or don't. My sister and I have already lost half of our blood, will never be whole. There can be no substitutes.

It's not us, we have to be assured.

Very early in life I'm aware of the consequences of being too close to my mother. I know if I successfully rid myself of the new man in her life, if I get him out of the house I live in for the time being, once she's older, she'll be lonely. There will be no one to take care of her. I will have to go back for her, if there is no other man in her life, see her through the rest of her years. Have to be the man of the house, again.

He will claim that he love us, the stepfather.

Some man is always claiming that. Or she says it for him, he loves you children.

He loves us. He loves us not.

He will always be a part of your life. He's a good man. Nothing like your father.

There are two family photos in the house we never live together as a family in. The house they buy after my sister and I leave home.

There we are, all four of us together in a photo op. Twice. He isn't my father. There are no pictures of my father, none in the house. None saved for some day. No reminders to flip through, remember he was here.

His image is ripped out, while my mother cries, tears, during a moment of strength. One day she returns home from work at the hospital, determined to excavate him completely.

My sister and I watch her cry, not understanding how you could want to just make somebody go away.

My stepfather didn't want his own kids, he told my mother. He had us.

My mother has to start taking up for us at work, her queer son and the white daughter who runs around with black boys.

In my family, every holiday becomes a reminder of how abnormal we are. We aren't what we are supposed to be. We keep trying to act like a family to keep away the hurt that will come at least once a year, every Christmas.

We don't know how to act like a family, though. We separate into our rooms. My mother cries, why can't one day be special? Just one day. No fights for once. What do we expect, why do we hate, why are our feelings constantly hurting each other, have to?

What are we waiting for? What are we expecting to make it all stop? What will make it go away?

In that house, constantly trying to second guess the correct thing to say in order to keep some semblance of unity. Our family, familiar.

Brian C. He falls asleep at school because he's been working so hard to save money to get away. On the floor, in the carpeted halls. Under lockers. I want to sprawl like that body. I imagine what it would be like to have my hands under clothes that touch his body, to be accepted by him, the only once to be accepted by.

He will wear a white dress shirt, no jacket, only white. White to be written on, in all yearbook pictures.

His chest would be thin, smooth. If I saw it. I've seen it. We're undressing backstage. I never make advances. He cultivates a casualness, Brian C.

He must know, he must see my eyes only wanting to move on in to him. The only pictures I want to cut out of the yearbook are his, the outsider, outside even the theater department. His eyes dark as his black hair, all points of light converging to, I long for, sweep over me, giving him my coloring, blushing.

My eyes, be mine. Nothing could be better than to lie down with what is him, that connection, to accept it in the only way I can, taking him into my body. Eating him. It's too easy to get lost in a woman's body, give him mine to hide in, he'd enjoy it. The struggle. He could confront himself in me.

He has problems with his mother, too.

All of my possible lovers could be dimmed by this vanishing into where I come from. If only Brian would take me. I'd be more like him, then, moved more towards what I want to be, Brian's. More of myself, haunted, wasted away.

I don't see him as having parents, like all of the other boyfriends who make easy marriages. He's more of an orphan, has more of a need for something, anything more. Like me.

I first see him in a One-Act school play, the first function I attend moving up to the next grade which is high school. With his presence, an actor, he's confident, changing, a messenger. He sings unlike me and is loved for all his talents, the lark quality he possesses.

Loved by our coach, the casting director. All the other students are tanned and fed, in good health, believe in all that, it just comes naturally to them. Whereas Brian shows the shortage of this with a bright pale, obviously foiling it, all his need, he is full of.

Something to look for, stand in the shadows of.

Trying to be near him swallows me, all of my concentration goes only to him. And I am focused with that challenge. It saves me, buoys me through years and days. He becomes my lesson in want, is my want, my only.

Brian C. stops believing in even the theater and the ability of his own talents to satisfy. He becomes the inverse of himself, his own compliment. He's no longer able to smile at the trivial that is our schooling, postponement of the inevitable disappointment our lives will be, if we stay here where they raise us to be held back, hold ourselves back.

No one challenges him, is worth his troubles. Not Brian. He stops showing up for rehearsals and auditions.

I think he goes to the closer college, when it's his time, but it's no use. Or it's too expensive. He quits, falls sick.

I think he's dying, wants to step out so far, get so far, far away, more. More away. Into death, even. He is sick of everything that is growing, grows so indoctrinated in our small circle, a one street city with its main drag. Poisoned, pointless, so fateless. Finally in a line we follow. You graduate, get a car. Order, all fenced in around us. So and so marries so and so.

I am watching him die. It is compelling, like we are halves of the same breaking in two, my eyes, outside of that, past all of this everything. We can survive death, even. We tempt it to take us in the middle of the night.

It doesn't dare.

He stops thinking of his looks, Brian C. He leaves it up to himself to keep going, get out, get out of here, this hell that is home, prove to the world that what I see, what everyone once did and then gave up on, eventually lost track of, is there. It's there in him. Where a part of me I can't even locate rests. I live somewhere deep inside of him, I know it.

He goes to my high school, then moves away. Then further.

Even when he was still in school, you could see him moving, preparing to move away from everything around him. Dropping out of sight, out of where he was arbitrarily placed.

Blue eyes, black hair. 1991.

His last year was the year I was one below. He is fair, the lightest markings on skin.

Handsome, skinny.

Androgynous.

A goofy smile, crooked, dog-eared.

The grin bursts, then his face clouds over.

His face recedes, he sits on the floors of hallways, under and between lockers.

His strong tenor, singing voice, honey that climbs pouring, a backwards purr, and moan.

We will hold people in common, common people.

Our drama coach is fascinated by Brian but has nothing but contempt for me. Even in that sector, that segment of outcasts, as the runt of the litter, I am struggling to assert myself.

Our teacher lives in a nice house, in the nice section of town, so far out from me you must drive to it. Out among the homes of hospital supervisors, parents of my sister's rich, white friends with curving driveways.

Before my sister's and their daughters' desires twist, roads with shaded greens on sides and sides. Whispering, beckoning.

We all go over, the entire drama troupe for the annual Christmas party.

I only remember one, the one after Brian C. had gone. Maybe you only got to go once you were a Senior.

We gather around bowls of chips, exchange wrapped gifts, present our teacher with tickets to a show on Broadway, plaque flowers or roses. His roommate Gene is like his husband, his life partner. Old, too. Apparently he has his own room in the house. Or it's the guest bedroom. That's what we whisper about and try to peek into, what normally goes on behind their closed doors.

I am discouraged with my hope for Brian.

I want to take Brian to the place where we will cease being ourselves intently, so intensely that we'll be lost, jarred by the immensity of how far we've come.

I'd like to have him with me the first time I ever make love, so he rides over all and becomes my first, sees, witnesses me. My first true love, loves me because I show him who I can be, one day. I see who he can be.

Before I stop letting him be for me, and move on myself.

I want to see him in his most vulnerable materialization, that manifestation, the stripped boy who must look up now that he's naked and knows he's being seen. And wonders what we see in him.

Or he closes his eyes tighter, so I can kiss wherever I want on, wherever my lips set down, land, kiss and make better marking it all the more consuming.

Pleasure that is so close to home, relative in its relaxing.

I see him as a projections of my self, a shadow to follow. I want to drop out of the tract like he does, become obviously disillusioned.

He stops worrying about dress, or huddles that group in the halls of our school. It's easier to just exist than attempt welcome, place. He comes to school less and less, leaves early and earlier in the day. Drives his beat up car, then truck. He gets it for himself because he works so hard. Saves up.

His white t-shirt or Mickey Mouse, baseball cap covers unkempt hair.

I run my fingers over the pages in my notebook, his picture in the yearbook.

His skinny frame saunters by, he looks down as he is walking forward, daring to keep going, giving up on here and now. Most of the other kids are concerned with the immediate and eventually wake lost. Brian and I plan ahead. Outside enough to see the road.

After he graduates I stay back in the drama troupe for a year trying to fill his role. The principal calls me into his office after a particular literary meeting we are bussed to. There've been complaints and rumors. Do I know what they're saying? That I was putting some boy in my mouth on the bus on the way coming back in front of everyone. B., my boyfriend.

It's not true. I'm inappropriate, my presence is disturbing others, the other students who shouldn't have to be subjected to me, I'm told. Everyone sees me, sees what I'm doing and have done. What I stand for. I will have to answer. I will have to leave here, be forced to if this ever happens again. The principal will call my parents and make them more aware of me and my particular deviance.

Brian C.'s body is skinny, boyish. His skin I imagine is as pale as that of some gill I could breathe upon, life into the only fish I want to catch, bass that flips and kicks out at air, until dying and then cleaned.

I imagine lying upon him.

He makes you want to occupy his aloofness, to be the object of his intensity, mental scrutiny wrestling with the surest way to proceed. There must be a way, to produce the fullest, most satisfying results.

My affections beam after him.

But I'm not the younger freshman he takes under his wing. I'm not innocent enough for that, for his vocal instructions, teaching. I can't sing so I will never soar to the head of our troop, commanding through unspoken notes like Brian and the freshman he goes off in private with to talk. There are rumors among us that they could be lovers.

Brian and I are only alone in private once. He keeps a distance. Only once when I'm homeless with a boy I run with in high school, then I get to see Brian in his bedroom.

We are being driven around a town on the outskirts of our own, the city thirty minutes away. My boyfriend is named B. I'm picked up from work. B. arranges for a mutual friend to drive us to find some place to sleep for the night.

She knows where Brian C. lives, where he has moved out to after high school. She idles in the road, with my boyfriend in the car and me in the car.

She goes up and knocks.

Then I go up and knock. No one is home and so back down, waiting in the car, driving around some more, coming back.

My boyfriend and I are all over each other, kissing in the back seat of the car parked in front of Brian C.'s place again, the friend watching in the front, then not so interested.

Brian knocks on a window. What are we doing in the middle of his street? Making out in public, in the broad daylight.

I get to go up and be alone with him in his room, a single spare in some old building. There's something I need to talk to him about.

Or I've come back another day in my own car. Now that I know where it is.

He has friends coming over, two women who are involved. He's also involved with them. I'll be going, then, before they get there.

I guess I can't stay there. Maybe if it was just me who needed a place. But my boyfriend and I can't stay there, not just for one night.

At first my mother doesn't know about my boyfriends.

But she is studying her community college course at the kitchen table. She sees me disappear into my bedroom, close the door, pull the phone in there, cord under the door.

I start dialing out, looking to be met, to be kept. I talk low in the room, a small argument starts building into someone else is leaving me. The phone hung up, slammed, rings back. Waiting for his mind to change, my boyfriend. Never will. His cooperation is not. Never. I hang up the phone again.

He ceases to exist for me. If I can cut off my father, I can certainly cut off him. He won't, won't, doesn't care. He isn't taking care of my emotions. My mother suddenly gleans it all over studying.

Her boy is not friends with the other boys, particularly this very one. The boy on the phone and her son, they aren't friends. They

22

are more. On their way to a life of furnished, filthy apartments, shabby dwellings.

I refuse to fight about it.

I should at least be entitled to my own feelings, since they're all I have.

The stepfather has to swear never to lay a hand on me. The moment he touches me, I am out the door. I tell my mother.

Silence will strain until ignorance breaks out, the need to vent no longer ignored, will no longer be, damn the consequences. He throws me into my room. He picks up a black dancing cane from a school play I was in, the glitter tip cracked over my head. Repeatedly he begins striking me. Over my head it cracks over me until I fall down in a corner beside my dresser. Next to the glow in the dark orange pylon I stole from the road, a decoration. My touch.

I lay there until I find strength to fight back. I don't know where it comes from. I say I'm leaving.

I told him he could never hit me. I told him that.

He broke his side of the deal, so my mother has to suffer. He's the same father who thought it was ridiculous for me to have that calendar of women in swimsuits, oiled, tacked up on my door behind my weight bench.

She's the same mother who went through my underwear and sock drawer and found those books of erotica, before I really had anything to hide, anything to even be ashamed of.

I say I'm leaving. I tell my mother I hate her husband. I won't come back until we can talk rationally, until we can live like adults if we are going to be under the same roof. It isn't up for discussion. I have to look out for my self if nothing else is going to. She has to understand.

Next door to where he was hitting me so much, many times, throwing me around, my sister cries. From embarrassment, not from concern for me. She quotes the bible, some saying like that was historical fact, not just another book.

How could I feel anything God doesn't want me to feel? I yell at my sister, the sister I was there for, trying to shut her up. I'm still your brother. But at that moment I'm not.

All there is is yelling. Yelling right and left. There is no rationale to it, because every side counters another in this rising that is our house.

Our home finally breaks.

Soon, they'll all known what my sister does too.

There are fights, always fights. Every day now. Day, night, before and after supper.

Just like the constant fights in the black school I grow up in, school where my sister can choose from any number of men. Mother tells her now she will never get married, never have a white boyfriend. They don't want girls who have gone with black boys, lain with them, been touched by them. That's what my mother says.

My sister doesn't care. She says if that's the case, so. My mother cries. Where did she go wrong? How did she fail so miserably raising us? Her two kids won't grow up to be something her parents can be proud of. They're stupid, anyway, my sister says. All white boys, all boys the color of our absent father.

Blank.

If that's how they feel, she cries.

Trying to shake her, my mother tells her they only want her body. All they care about is sex. Don't you know that? My sister says white boys don't like her, that they never pay her any attention. So it doesn't matter. My mother says, you know why that is.

Same for me. Me with older men, as old as my mother. One with a BMW, one with a Mercedes. Older, ruining my life, all my chances, my intelligence. My mother says, you were always smart, so brave.

Me who is going to die, who already could have died in the hospital, sick weakling the whole time I couldn't seem to adapt, grow up.

The one that has had a life under an oxygen tent, hooked up to a breathing machine. My mother doesn't want me in the house, not her house. Not her clean house. She doesn't even want me eating with the same silverware, off her plates. I might give them what I'm gonna get, give them the sickness I'm bound to die from. Kill them all, the entire family.

She says that, my mother who is supposed to be smart. My mother yells and throws silverware onto the floor, spilling out entire drawers of ordered trays. Spoons forks and knives land in a clatter when lead to believe they should so easily lay cooperating. I am slammed against the screened door by myself.

She's just scared, so scared. She doesn't want to have to watch me die one day. But already I know it's not just like the news. Know it's not just the sons who die.

My mother says she never had the chances we have. She had to raise us single-handedly, make sure food was on the table. Two men her

25

entire life, her first husband right out of high school, Dad. And then the second, the stepfather, who helped raise us. At least she has him, she says. He always loved us.

She doesn't want us to make the same mistakes she did, she says.

All she wants is for her children to be happy. She raised us the only way she knew how. Following her mother's example, the mother who since we were Catholic wanted her daughter to remain married forever. That's what you did in our religion, what your mother told you.

She doesn't see how we are doing as she's done, not as she says. Going agains the ill-logic of the mother, logic that is not going to allow us to keep living. You stayed married. No matter how many times he got drunk, no matter how abusive he'd become, no matter how many times he hit you, threw your children, the baby boy into the wall.

We are Catholic, were. If she gets a divorce, the family will never speak to her again, that's what they threaten, how we are damaged.

I don't want to hide anything from my mother. She should know she's not going to change my desires. Desire is all I have. It's all I can hold on to.

I can no longer bear to listen to my sister I once took up for. My mother and her were rolling on the bed, fist-fighting. She has gone as dumb as the rest of them. My mother's husband wrestles me away from the door, as my sister punches my mother in the face.

I won't live in this house, with this guilt. This family began too broken for me to ever buy that, that anyone here is any more the model to look up to.

I don't cry. I sit on the front steps, waiting for some man I meet through some boy I sleep with to come pick me up. To take me away, give me a place to live.

I say I won't talk about this. I say I won't.

I'm not going to discuss my desire with them. But things change. I'll get to move away eventually.

Let me tell you about B., the one who was my boyfriend in high school. The one I actually got to touch, and keep touching. The one I wanted to marry, as soon as I got out of high school.

We run away together, many times. I steal the savings bonds sent to me on every birthday by my grandparents on my mother's side. It's when I still have a key to the house and no one's home.

The bonds are locked away in a fireproof security box in my mother's bedroom. I cash them unmatured, enough money for a motel room a couple of nights.

I give B. my letterman's sweater, from academic achievements, the top ten percent of my class. I give him my class ring, silver. His parents hate me almost as much as mine hate him. But one day, many years later, his mother will come over to see mine, to return some of those possessions I leave behind with her son.

It's older men, ones who live thirty minutes and miles down the highway out of town, who see glimmers in me. I don't know why they like me and not my boyfriend I take with me in my car, sleep with when he doesn't have other plans.

One of these men sends me balloons where I work next door to him in the mall during high school and that first College break I go back for Christmas. He works with his older lover. They cut hair among women I perceive at first as sophisticated, later insecure. B. is jealous. Not of me, but of the man's attentions. He wants it. He wants the balloons sent to him. To come between couples, become the object found in long grass, placed between sheets.

I become threatening, able to tear apart homes.

B. won't talk to me, because men he'd like to invite him over call looking for me, to find out how to get in touch with me. I tell B. I won't call them back. Then he goes to that bar. I find him out wearing clothes I've left at his house when running away again so I can change before school the next day waiting to graduate. He's wearing glasses I like on him, mine. Out at the bar where I knew I'd find him. There he is. He pretends like one day he'll settle with me, just like he pretends to run away with me. It's all a game for him, but this is my only life.

One day he can't take it anymore, turns yellow-bellied, returns home after lying with me on the rug in one of our friends' boyfriend's apartment. B. pretended like he was running away with me, we'd get an apartment. Swearing love, he'd never leave. He's not leaving. He just misses his mother, his father and even the brother, wants to go back. I won't blame him, I swear. I'd go back to my own if I could. My stepfather says it's too late now. My stepfather says I made my bed. B. says he won't go if I don't understand. I absolve him, finding out later he wanted to pursue some other guy, that's the only reason he wanted to go live back at home with his parents. We don't talk after that.

Once there is nothing holding me there, no him, I will leave that place where I walked through school as soon as I can.

The man takes me to his house, miles away.

    The next morning he drives me back to the city for school before a final late bell. 8:30, everyone should be in homeroom now. Attendance taken. All of the kids I go to school with see the expensive car I'm dropped out of, gleam like a shiny silver knife morning, like the razor he buys for me. He prefers for me to shave.

    Into life I'm cut off from.

I knew what this man wanted. The night before he told me not to put my shirt back on. His morning plans have been laid out, and he knows he will make me stain it.

    When I talk to my mother on the phone, I tell her about him, a man who wants me, will drive me where I need to go, if she's not going to.

My mother calls me at the number I gave her just in case there was some emergency. She doesn't want to completely lose track of me. I'm staying with another man.

    He's not the only one I'm seeing.

My sister will run away. We are both periodically absent from high school for extended periods. I only see her at school if we both happen to be going that week, day. I hear about what she's doing, keeping herself, from other students who gossip us. That's another way we are joined. Two peas in a pod, my stepfather's garden.

I'm called out of class by the principal. They've found my sister. The principal has befriended her for her own good, had her in his office. He wants us to meet, my whole family, get it all out in the open. He is black man. In light of my sister, my stepfather doesn't want to look at him. He's gonna fix everything. My mother is called away from the hospital for an hour or so.

We're just going to get it all out in the open. Start all over again, as if that were possible with us.

My mother, I don't know what to do. My sister and I cry and hug goodbye until the next time we see each other, looking at the floor when the stepfather talks.

I don't want to see my mother like this. Nothing has been accomplished.

The principal says give your sister a hug. And the meeting is over.

Leaving the office I see my English teacher.

What are you doing? You're ruining your life by not coming to school. She was going to give me the Outstanding Achievement in English Award, but she can't now. My average keeps falling, if I don't come back to school, every day I miss.

I go back to school, staying there until graduation, at night with one of the men or in a hotel.

Rehearsal for high school graduation, walking across the stage. I'm mocked verbally by some boys in my class, all the hate they can find. Now that everybody knows. I hold my breath, waiting to leave the town and school behind.

During the actual ceremony, the principal skips my name when it's my turn to approach the stage. An accident. It could happen to anyone.

But it happens to me, standing off to the side of the line, letting the kids behind me go on ahead and get their rolled up pieces of paper, their names being called and not mine.

No need to venture further than the bar set aside for us.

B. disappears for entire weekends. Not even a call. I return to my high school on Mondays. I wait to drive him home after the 3:15 bell. I call the car our car, like that means something. Like we're married, partners or something. Like I could give him what my parents give me. Until they take the car away too.

My friends say I can do better than B., much better, I don't need him. I am more attractive, he doesn't treat me right, I could have anyone I wanted.

B. wants to be an actor, too. A year or two separates the bodies of boys. After a certain time, I wait to leave. That's all. I wait with hands folded. Pursue nothing else there where I was. Nobody around me can give me what I need.

I keep pocketing money, watching months fly. The day comes. And where I've lived and all of that finally ends, all becomes past.

I am closer to something, anything.

When was the last time, the last night? When did I finally give up?

I just stop going back, stop walking over, stop calling, leaving messages, writing notes, and wanting. Looking for him to have something to look for.

But count on him calling.

When he does, it's like I don't even hear his voice anymore. I am no longer threatened because I've been hurt more, deeper, completely. Always more. He is nothing compared to now.

We have nothing to talk about. Concerning him, it's over.

He calls periodically, following those numbers that pinpoint me. Lines stretched. Once I'm home in the middle of a movie, his voice. I've accidentally picked up the phone.

It's B., from high school. Your old boyfriend.

B., not Brian C. who would never call. For a second of hope I thought it might have been.

He calls the next year, leaves a message because I'm not home. Again the next, same thing. He calls again, same message almost exactly. Like nothing has changed in all the years. Why talk when I know what to expect?

Reports, when I return home for those brief periods.

B. was at the bar, the one and only. The one right outside our hometown.

In that poor excuse for a city. He was on stage in a dress, making his grotesque face. All he knows, "show-face" going on.

What does he want? To know I'm still alive. Can't answer. Bonds back then that tied me before. Continued contact will make me feeble. What's done is done.

Years later, at least six, maybe seven.

After high school. He calls again. A message, phone number. The area code he's close to home.

Call him collect even, just please call.

That place he will never be brave enough to run completely from.

B) My Education

I've been with two men and two boys. I'm eighteen, going on nineteen. I'm leaving home to go off to college. It's a natural part of life, a step in the right direction. Moving, I will no longer need anyone. I'll soon be nineteen, my whole life is in front of me. I'm determined to leave home, to go find someplace where I will want to live, forever, someplace I will never want to leave. Someone is out there I will want to be always with, won't want to leave. Somewhere I feel like I can live.

Some promise, hope.

I go from one part of the South to another.

Eighteen, I leave home like lots do. Going to where I feel like life can change, especially once I have finished college. My parents drop me with boxes, bags I've packed. All the clothes I want to keep. Throw the rest away. Blankets will be provided.

I will return home for a first Thanksgiving, but that's the only one. I go home for the first Christmas and the second after that, but after that I miss most.

When I do go home, I don't know where my parents live. While I am away, they move into a new house.

Some nights I panic deeply, calling my mother in the middle of those nights, waking her from deep sleep like an emergency. She worries about me. I am going away.

In a building full of strange bodies on all floors, I sleep. I am starting to know people my mother never will, will never see, never know anything about.

In Georgia, I'm at the state college. I live in the Graduate Dormitory, even though only a Freshman. My mother never went to college, and she was opposed to me attending this institution rather than the cheaper community college. The community college was closer. You can get the same degree. I have other plans. Set up as my guide a star.

I know he slumbers locally, low key. I hold him as the ideal man, an answer to my problems with boys so far.

My mind is set on motion, the notion of some supreme flight toward his scope. Getting away, achieving any inclination. It helps to think about him in the abstract.

But given time, my capture of him seems realistic achievement. Every day I get closer to getting further away. Further away from my mother, away from the base where The Air Force stations itself. From the magnolia tree in one of our four front yards.

In the dorm, I am still too restless. I can't sleep. I am alone. That's how it feels. Don't know the body of the boy across from me. I have a paper to write. I creep down to the lobby in the basement, a student lounge, turn on cable while all others sleep or go out drinking.

I see an image of him on television. He is being passed over a crowd by hands that support his body. I see traces of his lower hair where jeans are loose enough to fall away more, the loose elastic of snug, striped boxers in black and white and gray, his skin. I wait for an ideal. That moment. At the perfect time I reach my hand up and touch convex glass screen like I am touching flesh, more, halfway through completing my paper.

The sight of him. Then I can write.

Sleep, start falling into dreams where I am a famous actor he could love. Or a beautiful drowsy boy under confused hands to the direction of his accompanying.

Once I move from home, the meat on my bones dissolves. I get skinnier every day than I already was. I start living off of sugar. Cheap. My mom doesn't have money to support me. In glasses of water, I add as many packets of sugar as I can, the juice of a lemon wedge with free water, a plate of fries for dinner. I start telling the story about my freckles men notice. I fell asleep on the beach. Once, as a small child. When I woke, I'd been burned enough to cause peeling of my white skin and leave those dots across underneath.

I start in a higher English class, skipping ahead by a placement test. I know how to compose basic already. The younger teacher picks our reading list. Through her I become who I want to think I am already. We read D. H. Lawrence. She makes us keep a journal of our responses, reactions to everything we feel. How sexually charged Emily Dickinson really was.

I sit in the front under the lectern. Other students watch from the side. Once I oversleep, and I call the teacher to apologize.

My inability to sleep in a strange bed with the boy across from me wakes me in the middle of the night. Down two flights of floors, our room on the second. Out the heavy metal door I go into roaming over the different dark of the campus.

I walk waiting. Something is going to, something is going to happen to me. This same peace of wonderment again, an anticipation of greatness coming, impending fulfillment, I will never experience again once I realize one of the only reasons I ever came to school.

Feel that one particular man, whose street I mark on a map.

I know the name of the street. I put two and two together. One street on the campus leaves the page of the map. Connects to one joining one where I've heard of his living. His house. I follow my lead, walking from the campus. In night approaching morning, I try to see what house might be his. Might look like his might. Maybe he's home.

Can't find the back of one I suspect, lost in another row of houses turned.

But I see the lights, porch I'm certain are his.

Like in some song I imagine, red.

Joey was one of many roommates I had in the dorm. I felt closer to him than most of the men I lay with.

He had olive skin. I think of him and think of how he was never really there, in this state, never wanted to come far from his water where he grew up on beach. All these backwoods for him.

He wanted to go home, fond memories of somewhere left for worse. I wanted him here. Just wanted Joey to stay in the room with me, sleep deep, deeper, keep in the bed across from me with milkweed-like sheets and a darker blue color like water-top. Or water in a bottle, he is. His eyes milky blue, hair blond sand, thick swept back.

Classical books, and wanted to be a teacher, made me start to be like him so much I wanted to be anything he wanted to. Distance of romantic idealization between us. Once he goes, postcards come.

He goes from home to another place, beach or city. Feigns interest or really feels it, has heard all about what I'm up to. Remarkable that we were thrown together in that room, two faggots, both OK with it.

He's built classic, a Florida wine plantation, and his family's crest, behind him. He educates me what to look for. He knew this boy in class was because of this and that.

We go dancing one of the first nights. He's my roommate, lives with me. Close proximity. He's beautiful. We are coming back down black streets all sweaty in air colder than our red bodies. I'm unlacing my sneakers and taking off wet socks on my room side. He wants to bring it up, say it now, he's gay.

He hopes I don't have a problem.

Me too.

He wears loose shorts that go down to caps of knees, dark vivid greens, blues, always solids. We listen to stereo. His shirts lighter whites, black shoes, European or London. Pale pink lips. His fingers thin and artistic, pads cotton brushes. Occasionally he casually touches me.

Under the covers I can hear him drop off to sleep, and I blush, wanting to dream in the same air with him.

We go for Chinese food on the corner. I have nowhere near as much money as his family. He tells his mother about me.

He makes friends before me. He is the one that sees where to go, where I'll meet all of my lovers following, other men I go out dancing with once Joey's gone.

He wins me a poster of the local star, the one who put the town on the map, a party where you listen to music before it's released. Like we are a couple at a fair. He's knocked over set-up milk bottles, blessed with the correct door number. We were thrown together.

I'm still so impressionable, still don't know how severely I can look.

I'm still dressing like a boy years younger than my actual age. Sixteen, fifteen, takable. Someone could snatch me, just hitting puberty, the motions of finding desire.

This creepy man notices the bone of my nose, how structure makes it jut assertively.

After this I am taken to his room with covered windows, walls tacked over with pictures illustrating medical cases of bloody mouths. Bloody mouths on the wall.

One night with him, and I don't cave in completely.

Quiet, for the family, the woman landlord who lives down the stairs under. Under his bed.

One night he sees me looking at the star. After that he says he won't disturb me. He just wanted to walk over and tell me how I looked in this light, strong and adorable, not yet captured.

They were on nodding bases, he and the star I'm watching.

Everyone here is on nodding bases. You smile at everyone, even after innocence that once made you look up from books with eyes bright, convinced it was safe.

Before he'd had you, tossed you back.

On your bed in circles of sheets of paper plans, charting progress, the rhythm of the see him, timing voyage to correspond with certain disappearances, myths out of feathers left, Icarus. Constructing wings. And such nonsense.

For the month or so of Christmas break, I go back to work at the record store.

I purchase a wooden box with his name carved into it, special packaging.

The disc inside, his song. Sigh. Watch TV for any signs of him. His face an image in a desert, recorded mirage. Is broadcast. His hand, reaching out for me. Like this is some sign telling me to take it, touch. I am on my knees on the floor in front of him. He dressed up in costume as a cowboy.

Light arranges, to shape a picture of him. And we connect. Our hands just happen to. There in the next frame. Skin against his recorded image.

His against mine.

Then he smiles. I can't believe what I've experienced.

The first boy whose body I ever slept with, his personality strange and not compelling, a different story.

I see him the one holiday I go back for. Last minute shopping with my mother and sister. The boy I haven't seen since that day I laid him over his bed, got on top of him that way, is there with his father.

His face pressed down into white sheets, clean in an adolescent room. His boyhood. His parents knew all about him, and me. They let me sleep over, let me climb up onto longer, taller body, back that one day to go inside of him.

I would have smiled at him and his father.

The stores all decorated, connected. On an escalator, he must see me. Must be home from college, too. The community college.

An indifference now, going down a level.

I am hurting him, but I keep on. He wants me to accomplish, keeping pushing way into him.

In his parents private bathroom, we shower together.

After that year, that summer, I left him. I told him never cry over me, make me feel guilty. Make this scene, this feel like anything it wasn't. Nothing.

Simply the burn of humiliation, chance.

As soon as he made me feel any sense of responsibility, the car was started. It was over, I was leaving. I had my whole life in front of me.

He was crying, begging me not to. Don't leave him.

I was, I was telling him.

Unless he could stop crying.

He was crying come back to try and get me to. So I did, a day or so, fucked him some more. Put him on his stomach, over his bed. His parents were away. I wanted to go as deep as possible, then went.

The day I finally leave the dorm, I have a desk filled up with various clippings of his star face. Angles cut from papers, scotch-taped down. I can any day open my drawer and there he is. Every time I look for a pencil, records forfeited in my move from the dormitory.

I am getting my own place.

I slept in the bed in the house and am aware of how the previous owner is no longer there. He left town, finished college, like you do.

I replace old curtains, move items left behind to a back corner of a kitchen cabinet.

Some nights I am so hungry I can't sleep. I don't make enough to eat well. I try to fill my stomach with cookies I buy at the quick-stop just up the street.

Nights I sleep on the mattress on the floor, the door to my bedroom open to a room opens onto a porch. The front door open. There's a yellow wooden painted screen door, listening for steps.

The worst was making days disappear in summer. I'm determined to become anything but what my upbringing would dictate. I train myself, open my eyes to how my heart pounds. Can't afford a fan, from home for good.

I spend entire days listening to music, I want, keeping to bed, vocals the only wave in summer, some instruments.

Summer vacation, second year, Sophomore. I don't go home to my parents. I go home to my own house, my body laid out over the bed, starting to be all mine.

As I strip it down, old bedsheets for curtains.

I go out dancing with other boys.

I could be mistaken, suddenly think I'm something because men notice me. I go to a bar that has dancing and aware of all the eyes on me, I look young. Twenty, nineteen.

How impressionable I am. Who to act like I am, in case he might be looking over. It's easy to try and look like the boys I see in magazines. Plus when I don't talk, a lot can be projected onto me.

I can become whatever he wants me, act the part. I learn how to touch each one in that way they want to be.

My books I carry help me arrive at certain things, be more than just some boy. I know how important love is, how a lasting union, deep marking is what I want more. I crave it. Few boys my age want this. There is no permanence in their unions because there is enough in their lives already. I only know if I keep on like they do, I will come out in the end in some desperate not knowing, now what.

When the lights have come up, I look at the boys who dance around me. Some affect my rate of beating, groom themselves carefully at a mirror, gaze at reflections. What's next, after this period of easy bliss? Their college years, the schedule of classes, the illusion of working along the path towards something settling.

I'm working a job cleaning dishes from tables at a place in the middle of downtown, stays open all night. It's the morning before he is going down to Florida for a funeral. I've gathered.

Friends see him off to his car. He'll drive. I try to wave at him through the window, although he doesn't know my name yet.

Maybe he sees me at the door looking out at him, bar towel in my hand.

He's wearing a hat. I recall clothes, but I could just remember what he had on that night he asked me if I wanted to invite him in.

If anybody needs me, it might be him.

There is always some part of life that will be empty. His friend had just been taken away. Death before us.

The boy I wanted to act like was a character with a certain sensitivity. He plays that in so many roles, emotion some director helps bring to surface, pulls up out of him.

He looked vulnerable, loving, and scared. Tangible, in some wound. There he is mortal. Touchable, coaxed forth.

His breath on the screen brings it all to life.

I would become his actor, the one he could bring home from the movies.

My clothes I left home in, the ones I wore in high school. They get dirty because I don't have the means to wash them. Once I looked cleaner because I had my mother.

I become paler, resting for nights. My hair parts down the middle. I think it looks more English. I've stopped wearing belts. I have one pair of shoes, Jack Purcell's, they last long.

Long hair, I feel more wild. We all go out dancing, almost every night, sweating together, everyone we live close by. I start seeing his face from the television. Through the crowd like I saw it outside the door. I can't afford to get my hair cut. I think I'm making an impression on him. Surely he must see me, dancing every night.

He must know I sleep with guys, knows one of the guys I sleep with. I watch him make a big production of kissing men, like he wants me to see, wants me to know. That I could approach him.

I meet him at the house of this guy I've waited for more from. In the bedroom, while the party continues in the other room, we have a conversation he probably wouldn't remember. The way we shook hands, how I tried to muster charming uninvolved in my obvious. I'm so excited.

He asks me how I'm doing. What I'm doing all alone.

I say I'm studying the books that line the wall of the party we're at. He asks me about Lawrence. He's never read, but he hears great things.

Yeah, I know about him from school.

Out at the bar where we dance he recognizes me. Someone says he likes my freckles, though they are less and less pronounced until one day fade completely.

In many ways, I'm going for a more natural look in my appearance. There's a certain kitten quality I want that only men, older, can seem to bring out of me as they handle me. I desire to be desired.

When he finally makes a move that cannot be seen as anything other than sexual, I hug him hello. He holds tightly onto me. His friend is the guy I'm with who doesn't say anything yet, just watches me get hugged like that. His friend and I are going out of the bar for awhile. Come back soon. We are, aren't we? After a drive, we say.

Once in the car, he tells me his friend wants to be my lover. He can tell.

How?

He just knows.

I don't believe him, don't think I can let myself, some star.

I wake up in one morning soon after that, and think of the star from the night before.

The night it happens, I go there, out dancing, knowing not so definitely that he'll be there, but if he happens to be there, I am in that state of mind, that setting where something could happen.

He is there. I say the music isn't going to get any better. He offers me a ride home.

He asks me if I want to invite him in.

I don't know what to do with him in the house. Tea. We sit in the kitchen, talk. It's cold, there's no heat in my half of the duplex. I turn on and leave the oven open, take a hot, scalding shower, my skin all red, every night that winter, no heater. I throw on long johns and socks to keep my body temperature quickly into under all the blankets on the bed. I tell him this is how I cope.

Can he watch me do it? Watch me shower, if I will allow him to enter this ritual.

And I agree, taken already by him, he can.

He can do whatever he likes. I'm extremely nervous, take him into the bedroom, and recall trembling.

You must understand, even though he asked me if I wanted to lay down, even though we did, though we got into bed together, and held each and kissed, a bit, our lips brushing, we hadn't slept together yet.

The rush of my excitement I am forced to keep quiet, waking into his arms, next to his, lips next to my ears saying he can't sleep over, can't stay all night, has to leave before morning. Has a house guest to get back to.

He doesn't want to admit for some reason he could possibly fall asleep in my arms. He thinks he has to go home, that he can't stay with me, just having sex with me. He can't stay all night. That first night, second, third night, fourth. Tells me he's just going to rest a few seconds. Seconds turn into a couple of hours. More of the night, before going. Tucking me in before he goes.

There is a television at the foot of my bed. Before I sell it, before I move out of the first house, we watch videos. I fall asleep in his lap. One unconscious while the other is wide or just barely awake, touching the other. Lightly, he will stroke my hair, love it. This could be right before he shaves his. I don't comment. Both of our stomachs growl in response to being close. Hunger response to our touching, our laying over. Especially when very excited.

Another night he comes in. This after he has taken me out to the movies with him, politely asked about my family. He must know I have nowhere to go for Thanksgiving. I'm not going home for some reason. I'll be here, I tell him, for Thanksgiving. Not going anywhere.

The alarm I've set for five o'clock in the morning or so, before dawn even, so he can return home to his house, goes off. To feed the dogs. I try to wake him, tell him it's now that time, gotten there while he was just resting for a second.

He will slowly wake by my whispering gently to him, then fall back asleep, going back down into my bed.

I help him sit up, he's so tired. Says just a second, he's getting up, back down onto the mattress, longer with me, longer than he planned.

This makes me extremely happy. Makes me feel accomplished.

My lover is still saying he can't stay all night with me.

His body is ideal. Thin, strong. Sleek, swimmer's. We are almost perfectly matched. Only his is a bit bigger, I feel. He never sees it this way, always compliments. His compliments are always coming. He is always asking me are you happy? Always saying I am, with him.

He's wearing baggy jeans. We make love in the dark. I respond. We roll all over each other, on top of each other. When we are done we laugh once the fever of touching has broke, glad, exhausted with each other. Happy. He asks again to make sure. Yes. Sure.

Are you?

Yes.

When I return to school, I have finals. Walk to school in cold. His friend is here, the one who will later die, one of the ones. Many people die when I am with him, his grandmother, more stars. One morning after I'd lost my red glove, must have fallen out of my coat pocket. I couldn't find it during my walk to Italian class. My lover told me not to worry, he'd buy me a new one. Red gloves aren't that hard to come by. His friend just looked at me. Keeping his little girl, a baby, pushing her in a stroller.

I remember snatches of Italian I was learning, plus the baby stroller. The baby is a girl and looks removed already, blank.

Nights before his, we are still in my house. We touch, make love, hours. He is still feeling me out, deciding whether or not he really wants me. Or just someone. We will kiss in dark, go over and over each other's bodies, again. Try a little more, to dare a little more, touch more explicitly, low.

Pull back, kiss. And rest before starting back.

Go over it again, longer, more.

Kissing each other with open eyes, looking, face, each other's body, into each other. Our feelings touch.

Before he takes me to his main house, he takes me to a small guest cabin he has, asking me if I want to go there. After nights together in the cold. My bed, my house.

I was so happy I was being taken away, from my house down the street from his. It's at the bottom of a hill, where I live.

There are condoms. That's why I think it must have been the first real night. Because there never were before, and he's paranoid about that.

Just me coming to him, under his hand, still in my jeans.

As usual, it's extremely late. After last call when he's come by for me. He is asking me if I think it's too much, his wealth, obvious, all the houses for one man. All he has to show me. His friend who will later kill himself has left the guest cabin. He was here for those nights my lover spent in my house. Those nights when he had to get back before morning. He needed to check on him.

We must have gone to the cabin soon after his friend left, I realize.

In the cabin, two rooms with beds. Did he have any idea which room his friend stayed in? Which bed he slept in?

The condoms are rubber, almost yellow.

We each wear one.

Thin, they are, so you can still feel through to each other.

Our hearts fill. We pull at each other, on our knees, in the bed. The other bedroom of the cabin is empty, quiet and dark. The barrier sliding giving. I rub up and down in my hand.

Under me. Underneath, he is warm and hot.

We wash up, throwing the used condoms now knotted into the trash can somebody will empty later and find evidence. This is the first time I've ever worn one. I've had other guys. He insists I protect myself against him, vice-versa.

Delicately, and of course I don't resist.

A painting in the room, on the floor propped up against wall.

He shudders when he comes, lets me make him.

We may have slept in the bed his friend spent one of his last nights in.

There's no way to really know.

He wants me to get tested, just a precaution.

I go. He pays for it, a little extra left over from the bundle I can keep.

The day of the test, he is meeting with his printer. My lover takes pictures, always meeting with someone.

Why don't I talk more?

I tell him how I vowed to come for him, to find him, that I'd get him. He wants to know is this how I thought it would be?

He thinks I've been hurt deeply, that no one should go through what I've gone through.

I can't be possessive. What I can get from him must be all I need. Busy man. He says he is being completely honest.

We go back to his house, sleep there. Can't stop. When he is here, we have dinner together.

Almost twenty.

My boy body pressed against his frame. I learn where to touch him, where he wants me to, how he wants me to touch my own nipples for him. My bedroom personality, coming up against him, what he likes. Feel myself pleasing him. Alike, lovers. He sees so much of me in him, this scares him. He went for an entire year once without really talking to anyone.

There he is. I tell my mother, because who else can I?

I see him more than I see my family.

When I'm in school, I go through classes knowing I have him to return to, recording in my notebook, composition books, in so many words or less.

For years I go in the morning to school. I want to stay with him, in his bed. I have my own bed when he isn't around, isn't in town.

He is scared he isn't enough for me. When he can't take me whenever I'd like, has to go away, leave, afraid that I will just be frustrated and go sleep with someone else. Afraid to leave me frustrated.

Hearing this is enough to keep me faithful.

He knows I'm young, my hormones all out of balance, that I always want more.

He asks if I've told my mother. I had to tell someone.

He seems glad.

I felt I loved him quickly. But I had to watch myself, for I knew how he felt, how he tended to regard those in my position, boys or girls, never with love. His long bouts of celibacy attracted and excited me, that he could cultivate intensity. I knew also he had another lover at first, a woman in New York. I sleep with him every night he is here.

He would talk. Say all he'd seen, parties, famous people, the dinners, lunches, the amazing restaurant he was at. You can't believe this place, he calls me from.

Before I'd given over to him, quit my job, my friends. I'd be in my apartment, at my desk, waiting for him to call, say he was done at the bars. Did I want to see him? Could he come get me?

That night, every night.

I go on sleeping beside him, his warmth. Laugh, he knows I haven't been eating when he isn't here, traveling elsewhere.

He wants me to take a job, so I'll be able to eat without relying on him, be stable without him, not in such constant terror of hunger. Trying to make ends meet when he isn't here to help.

He leaves many times. It's part of his job description, part of who he is. He reminds me of that. I knew who I was getting involved with, he says.

Although in the beginning he has another lover, he wants himself to be enough for me. He says he thought I would let the other guys go. I would want only him, immediately. It doesn't take me long.

I learn his body, how to hold, touch, place it next to mine. His body above mine, and under it. Let it be touched. Talk to him, more. I don't talk enough. I'm quiet.

He wants me to tell him about others, lovers, times.

I want to be there for him but he is far away. He will always be going.

He goes away, to do work. Work takes him. I have to stay at a certain safe distance. I have to approximate the filling he has in life outside me.

He is in Florida. Miami. Different from where we go later for some wedding.

Pre-production of a recording for him, one of many.

He sends a picture. Him in expensive glasses and a daring coat has fur-lined trim around collar and neck. Black and white Polaroid a friend took of him. A friend there with him.

I slide the picture into one of the composition books I use while going to school.

His mugging for me.

But maybe not. Maybe he saw his face and thought of me, then sent it. He wanted me to see him like that.

He had to have that year, that going through one without talking to anyone to get him where he was today. All the people who want to talk to him, versions of me.

One of the times he's gone away, someone else has died.

I hear about death that is important enough to come as news on television. I call a number he has given me. I am worried about him, call the number to get in touch with him. I am concerned about how he must be taking the news.

I'm not able to reach him.

I hear he is at the funeral.

Then I see him on television, his suggestions for mourning.

Before I hear from him. So early on.

He will say I never said the right thing about this death, was never there for him when he was far away and needed me. Never consoled appropriately. I tried to call, I had no idea what to say, how to respond to emotion that wasn't mine. I had no idea how he would want me to, what would be too much, too little.

There is some part of life that will always be empty.

Another death, another friend.

I learn I can at least be there for him when friends die.

I thought I could become a husband.

He told me I had what I wanted, when I told him how I told everyone I was going to go away and find and marry him. He adds our last names together with a hyphen, spoken in privacy. In the morning, late at night, I sit beside him in my own chair in his kitchen.

He pretends we put up a Christmas tree together. I answer his phone occasionally, but always feel he'd rather I didn't.

He talks about his emotions as someone else's. He says don't confuse the singer with his songs.

Certain things are not for me, certain parts of his enormous life.

He cries at little things, because he wants to let people see him cry.

He's a public figure and all, I know this. To not expect too much of him.

Like a boy, I love him. He is a grown man. Closer in age to my mother than me. When I talk about members of my family, he feels closer to me. I know that he's used to much more than me. He'll never even have to look for certain things in me.

He says he's been true to me. Girls, boys, women and men throw themselves at him. Invite him up to apartments. Or for weekends. They're just friends. No reason I should feel threatened, no reason at all. Often, I'm being unreasonable.

When I question him and this one particular woman, I've crossed a line. How dare I? Some woman, another one of his friends.

To not believe there's goodness where he sees what he does. How could I be wary of someone he trusts? He likes, has allowed to be his friend. Someone who will be connected. Again and again, in this magazine and picture, this paper and book.

Someone he will let exist in a way I never do.

Instead of feeling at home where he lives, I look for signs of my exclusion, how I could be more involved with him.

I just want more and more to hold onto, grasp. I'll grow out of this confusion of so much. I know how he thinks I'm smart, how he fears his own stupidity.

Just because he didn't finish school, like that means anything, in this day and age.

He watches me shower.

It could be early morning, late night. Whenever he has time, and I'm bathing in his tub. When he still likes to see me there.

Sometimes hands me a towel, wraps me up in it, watches me washing. I borrow clean bright pajamas from his closet.

Those hours he would have a cigarette before bed, there's no robe for me to wrap myself up in like one of each and everything in hotels we sometimes stay.

I try to keep myself company, when he has retreated into his career and I'm back in my apartment. I don't really live with him. I read. Whenever he isn't here.

There must be other people in my life I can see.

There's no one in my bed, in my room.

My love makes me stubborn. I'm in his house, but it's not my house.

While he is recording, I write him letters in the form of books.

I wish he would call, wish I would know he accepts me, who I am.

Especially after the last time we talked. I told him I felt like he was fucking with me. He said he'd call me back. Maybe I said too much. I hope he keeps me.

He has clean towels and clean sheets. When he leaves, I know I will not have what he's given me. I can't afford any of it myself. There will be all the other things to consider, too.

To just look at him arouses everything. I'm lonely for him. How much I want him. In countless ways I tell him.

He says I seduced him. I try so hard to make it last. I'd often underestimated myself. He was proof of what I could accomplish.

I just have to keep my wits and looks about me. Charm, my heart. Whatever it is he likes about me. Wants my body, heat, and he says I'm beautiful. Just wait, one day they will be knocking down my door. He tells me there are so many people who see how incredible I am. Just give them the chance.

I don't like when he talks like this, like there is bound to be someone else at some point, an end to us.

I age so much with him. See only him. Want only him. Everywhere, him all over me.

In this picture my mother comes to visit in the apartment I've got for myself. My hair is long and curly.

My sister is also visiting.

There is a map of the world behind the couch we sit on, arms around each other, a map of the world. I've tacked it against the white wall. My mother has come to accept me, even though she has no actual proof of the lover's existence. Maybe she believes me. Soon enough she'll see for herself. I'll leave the country with him.

He's not around today. He's gone to sunny California, the first place he flies me out to.

The only other time I remember being on a plane was with my mother and sister. A contest to see who got to sit closest to our mother. We were coming back from a visit out to family on my mother's side, the only side we knew, and the plane shook. She told us to close our eyes and pray, though we didn't still go to church. She was remarried now, and the new husband didn't go, on the trip, or to church, with us.

C) The World

A little more than a year after the first night, he goes off for an extended tour. Occasionally, I'll be able to go wherever his work takes him. One of these trips takes me out of the country for the first time ever, to join his tour.

He wakes me that morning before his trip, a long time away from each other, longest yet. Maybe he'll never feel the same again, once he gets back. You never can tell.

He drives me back to the apartment I rent, and he tells me to think about him.

He says he'll be thinking about me.

Vacated, emptiness in this place will never be that sharp again, it just dulls everything. Around me. I have a long wait ahead of me. A year that will feel like a yearning already.

This initial pricking in my heart, swelling panic, like now he's gone and has left. There is no way to get him back.

He enters me deeper than even my father leaving me.

Heart beats to strokes he pushes into me, I count how many times before it is done.

I know he's going. I've always known that, that he would go.

He's at a picnic table. Figs are falling from trees they are so plentiful. He is calling me from somewhere.

He flies me out and I start to travel. He gives me money to spend. Play money, he says. Spend it all there, wherever we are.

Before I leave.

I try to stay longer.

In California, he rents me a car. Not since high school have I driven.

We almost always at night touch each other.

Views from our hotel rooms.

We sit on the couch in one hotel and he cries with his arm around me. I've put on an album from his childhood. Before his life became this dream.

We are holding each other.

He says come over here, and he puts his arm around me. They're happy tears for him.

In that hotel where he always stays, he is hearing his past means something to him. The song about what a boy does when his father dies, how he dreams of recapturing that father's body before it left.

It touches him. I am there, sharing this moment with.

I try to imagine what it could possibly mean to him, this song.

I start to think I can reach him, just by thinking about him. That I can figure out exactly what he wants, doesn't say, if I pay close enough attention, and try to be just what he wants.

If I contain seeds for songs.

That boy, beauty, he sees.

California, 1994. I was in the place of the dead boy. We went to where he died on the sidewalk. My lover shakes the owner of the club's hand when we go inside and have a drink, meet some actors, screenplay writers. Right outside is where the boy hit the ground.

I'm wearing a fancy coat of his, because it gets cold at night and I didn't know. I hadn't packed properly for the desert.

My lover was still only feeling out how realistic his future, further career goals were. He wanted to start making movies, meet lots of people that could help him do that.

I will have no one to call out to when I feel like he has trapped me in strangeness. This feeling is through my own fault. California I have no part in. I'm only there to see him, my only purpose. I will collapse.

I send a postcard from that hotel room to some other contact I need.

I can't let him be everything, because he is unsure.

He takes over everything. That vastness is his.

It will never be easy to move on. I've shown him. This nice hotel room, luxury, too much need. As I grasp for him. I have.

He says he realized this one night. I ran out onto the balcony, cried because he couldn't hold me exactly how he opened me, made me feel I needed to be contained, entered by him, how dangerous this was. I have no business with someone like him.

There is more. There are a number of other nights like these, many more.

The boy in the blue sockhat in a place that is completely unfamiliar.

I have become someone else. He tells me to look around.

I sit down and wait on the wharf, Switzerland. We have ice cream cones. I rely solely on him, my only familiar.

He wants me here. We take the boat over to France. He gives me foreign money. He met me at the airport and we rode a train that took us to the pier, the lake where the boat will take us over to mountains. The hotel is high up in them.

He tells me about Paris, how he spent his time when, the fashion shows he went to. There is cold but there is sun.

I fall asleep against him. The excitement exhausts me. A food tray brought through, sandwiches, for sale in a foreign language.

We check into the hotel. Arrangements are such that I'm registered as being in a room with his friend here and not his. After the initial panic, insult, he takes me aside to confirm my place. I settle down in his room.

The lawyer arranged for the rooms. I don't want to put my baggage down in front of the lawyer, not a second.

My lover's suite, I place myself on the bed, waiting for the lawyer to leave. Leave us alone.

That night we will be having the first of many elaborate meals, rich food.

Out our window, over balcony, you can see another country across the lake, mountains of Switzerland. We are across in a resort hotel.

Snow in the mountains, none on the ground.

The vastness of space plays with my mind.

We have late night meetings in the lobby. The men he works with, their wives, girlfriends, families, some of their friends, my lover, me.

We are in the middle of this stressful situation for the band of travelers. A sudden change of plans I'm brought into. We will be staying for awhile rather than hitting stops originally planned. Everyone my lover is traveling with needs to rest.

Once together, everything. Is only part of what he sees.
How I start loving him.
He takes me away where it's strange I want to live and never come back.
Across the world in winter to summer somewhere else.

I see Europe because of him. We are happy together in the boat that ferries you across Lake Geneva. He wants to buy me whatever I want. He gets sick a couple of times.
I have to leave him in bed in the hotel, even though I'd stay. He wants me to go off with men he works with and their wives, lovers, their families we are vacationing with.
They are all going skiing.

With cameras that are cardboard boxes you throw away when finished, film developed, thought carried over, you have moved through time.
Into an image, through glass window, plastic of the shutter.
Shuddering, I snap a memory of our surroundings, as many as I can muster to document, try and duplicate.

Words exchanged, changing sheets, the sun greeted. Breakfast taken together as dreams intermingle in telling them. Back into bed together, into those same knowledgeable arms.

Rooms, worlds only accessible to me through him.

As I am being lead, shaped, still struggling to find form under him. I cry when he goes away. He has to.

The balcony at The Chateau, overlooking the valley. Lights, the basin.
The mountain in Switzerland, courtyard, body of water, joint showers.
The glass and chrome, gold fixtures.
It is so marking, the way he comes into me, rushes.

Friends are waiting in the lobby. I've dressed but it doesn't matter what I wear. He is with me, on my arm. I am his accessory. We compliment each other.

We were playing a drawing game in the lobby, with all the guys he works with and makes money with, responsible for these vacations. He kept drinking because of the stress, my lover. Someone else was sick. Another concern on his shoulder I reached out to put a hand on, tried to massage. Sometimes he brushes me off.
At first we were winning every round of the game. How in sync we were. He knew what I was going to draw, words I was going to try to get him to say before I even put my pencil to paper.
Then his eyes got blood-shot.
Something was ripping deep down inside him, his body breaking, emotions unchartered.
Then he would become cruel, regularly insult when he got like this. Felt uncomfortable enough as it was.

The time comes for us to leave. There is the phone, or meeting, or calendar, or agenda.

We must leave the hotel and bed. There are other places to go.

On his tour bus, planes, on his account, I go. I try to nest inside him. All the different bundles of sheets I slide into, rise up out of. He tells me to look out the window. We are in New York, look. My first sight of many lights, the vast difference between worlds. The world is so big. His hand in mine bridges it. Hotel lobbies, expensive dinners, menus. I am at his side. Conversations happen. I gradually learn more and more, learn to be less intimidated.

Still, there are many whose faces I don't like, or hearts I don't, words, voices, thoughts, concerns. All these people I must learn to tolerate.

The supermodels are a major problem for me to sit across from.
Because what am I? Nothing.
Just his lover, a boy.
Sitting there, for no reason. Just to be with him. Everybody knows what he thinks about love.

I have been to many places so quickly with him I'm no longer sure I even speak English correctly.
London, I am afraid of the waiters.
I am there down at the other end of the table. He wants me to be as content as if we were married. We aren't, and I fear that.
We are two men, and I the lesser.
The younger, poor one, unknown. He is the one with a family.

I will write home about my trips between semesters and during holidays from study. My mother thinks both of her kids have grown up. From hotels, I call asking her to guess where I am. Wanting to love my family just like my lover does his.

A bigger vision of the world than I was born into.

I never thank him enough. I am never grateful enough because I never want him to think he's giving me exactly what I want. I don't want him to think he's met my needs, because he'll stop trying, think he's done enough for me. Then he'll get rid of me.

I am not his family. I can never forget that. I am not a given, a personality that must be reckoned with.

Once together in London, sleeping under the same roof in the hotel as his family.

We meet in the lobby, go out to dinner, then upstairs to a private room.

The meals, smiles shine.

His family is complete, full. Not like mine with just my mother and sister, the three of us with uneven visits.

He never goes with me to visit them, but he does see them if they happen to be here in town visiting me. A couple of meals together, he and I, my mother and sister. Or just my mother. Or mother and her husband, also.

They all know I am with him and what I do with him. I don't think he ever treats them, although he does more often than not pay for my dinners. An entire year or two I'm jobless.

There is the time my grandmother is here, too. I sit next to my poor grandmother who wants to treat my friend "Mike" she calls him. Not his name, but we don't correct her.

He is a perfect gentleman, helps her walk up a hill, back to the car after guiding her, lending support.

I know a little about when he ignored his family, left them behind because he had something to prove to himself. He was still young.

He once lived on spaghetti in a rat-infested basement. He caught one and set it on fire under the house. The smell of burning hair, flesh cooking, they never had a problem with rats again.

Soon the rumors will reach back to where I come from. No one will make fun of who I am, loving men, because he's not like any of them. I've been with someone who has more power than any of them ever will in their entire lives.

They will accept me, all because he loves me.

The lover sees himself in the boy, at that age.

I am 20 through 23, 24 even.

The lover says he never wants to bring age up, he never wants it to become an issue.

He says I'm smart. He loves my hair, always keep it long so he can run his fingers through.

The lover too had a father that went away.

But his father always came back, even when he went to war.

There has to be more than just bed between us, he schools.

We have to have more to give each other, come back to when we separate for those periods.

I don't want him to think I want anything else from him, that I care who he is.

Only that I want his body. His body is all.

He tries to teach me to be social, become friends with his friends. Like he would teach a child who doesn't know, only up to this point has fumbled. Born into this warmth of his, this wealth, richness.

He will openly admire the build of my body.

From this point on, he determines my self-esteem.

He fathers me, he mothers me.

I take my mother and her husband, my stepfather, into my lover's rich world. A glimpse of what I mostly live in. My stepfather is glad to be included, my mother glad she gets to meet my lover, develop a relationship with him. He's famous.

Even from the beginning, I count the days he is still my lover. I know what kind of man he is, what it means for him to be to me.

The kind of man who makes my mother and her husband feel welcome, whose family they meet, are pleasant together. His family almost feels like mine. My mother wants to talk again to his, meet them all again. She writes thank you letters to his family, and him, after the concert we all go to together.

I think of him as my maturing, becoming everything I want for myself. I go from boyfriends to my lover, him. Before there was nothing.

Lovers, that's what he calls us. We are lovers. But my boyfriend, too. Even though he hates that word. He says he's never had a boyfriend before, before me.

From now on, celebrity becomes something I question, human and full of faults. I want him to see I don't find any real importance in all of that, the other part of him he wants me to love. I can't, because there in that area he can leave me. I am so young. Too young, so unequal to fame.

I've captured the unattainable, and for that reason I feel anything is possible, accessible. Like I actually have a certain talent, ability even, have what I want. For awhile I think I might always be able to be this person, his lover.

They boy on his arm he beds among all his friends. They know. They all wait for that day, morning they know is coming. That morning I will no longer be there like that.

I smile, smile at them, all of them, won't let myself start to think of the day he's left me.

A day on the side of the road, where I become something that once was and now isn't his.

When I have him, anyone would think I should be happy. Since he's my lover, my partner.

Can we ever be equals? He's free. He's famous and has lots of money. He'll always be able to leave, take another trip out of town, get a house in the city.

I am some attachment, someone hanging on to him.

Everyone must see me like that, as some supplement to him.

Simple as that.

Can I be anything else? How can I, if I am with him? I start to see myself as seen. Why would he come to this person I've always been before? What's different now, makes me able to have this that is him? I am never easy. I feel I must prove my worth, I have something to offer, I'm someone, more than just some boy.

He could have any boy.

I act cold and set. Like maybe I'm sure of myself, don't need him.

What he wants to see. I must have my own reasons for liking him.

I only like his friends who see something in me despite him. Outside of that, see he's found something in me. Over dinner, those who feel I may have something equally interesting to say. So they listen to me. Mostly, though, it's his stories. We no longer go dancing. He frequents the bars.

I stay home and wait for him, at first.

Then I get lonely, want to join him, be with him more, before he leaves again.

I'd like for us to be alone. Repeatedly, I tell him. He's a busy man. His time is limited. A little for me, more for his friends, endless friends we entertain.

He wakes and sleeps with me. What more do I want?

He'll be out seeing friends late.

The bars close. He can't sleep, wide-awake, comes by to collect me. We return to his home until I get up and go.

In the college town when he leaves, his friends try to make me feel at home without him.

He never really comes back.

He keeps leaving so his return home after the tour won't be such a shock. He keeps going away, doesn't really have to live here, anywhere. At the beginning, we were both living this as our life.

Friends never talk about lack, how he divides himself between so many lives and roles.

Just the mere proximity, all his stories, excite them. He's whole enough for them. They can never get enough. He makes sure. He's a busy many. They all understand.

They never question his famous face. Behind his back, when he's away, they wage subtle wars for his affection, to see who gets to bask in his presence the longest. Who he'll call as soon as he gets back.

Bars, his home away from home.

I am not nearly near enough when beside him. Everyone else acts loud and funny because they're drunk. He loves to see everyone so drunk.

He hates more than anything being tied down. When he has no idea what I'm thinking. How he feels he can't reach me, I'm withdrawn.

He gets so drunk, stays. Especially once I start going to the bars with him. Since he doesn't have to come pick me up later he can get drunker. He passes out while I am kissing something unconscious, the thing he's become.

My mother says my father drank because he never wanted to grow up.

We go out to the bars, we go home, we have sex.

Up in the North, taking care of ridding herself of a first seed planted in her, my sister even recognizes some element of solace in my lover's marked face, voice, song. She is away one summer with my mother's parents. She's too young to grow up with a child. My grandparents don't know why she's there. They're glad to have her, though.

She needs time to heal.

Separated, my sister and I become fans of the same song of escape, his. She hears it too, even she. He has access to everybody through the radio, television.

My sister is never really comfortable with him, though. She cannot deal face to face with the vast greatness that is him. Mine, I tell her.

My lover. She will sit there and not look at him when she meets him. She isn't going to make some big deal out of him, let him be.

How could his feelings possibly be anything less than pure? What could he possibly be getting out of this relationship with me?

On the other hand, brother she knows wants nothing more than to escape, get away from every place they've ever been, ever lived. Every house, yard, their family's ever been in. Every year, bed.

What reason could I have besides all he could do for me?

Buried so completely in him, I think how I'll no longer have fresh towels or sheets, clean warm pajamas to sleep in, when he isn't with me. No longer sleep under arm. He won't bring me coffee in the morning as sun comes in through curtains, canvas, art stored all around us.

We roll ourselves into one.

We might as well live together, but don't. Get up out of bed. I walk home to start my day. He says he's an international superstar, has work to do. It's supposed to be a joke, but I don't laugh because I hate when he says things like this.

He is out in the world again. I return to my apartment. He's coming back soon, though, he says. I sleep on my couch when he is gone.

The couch left here by the boy who had the place before me. Like my mother did after my father left. Beds feel too big without bodies we're used to having there. Too big for just us. Like we could get lost in absence.

D) 3 Concrete Problems

1) Graduation

The lover I was waiting for, groom myself for.

I lie under him and think air will enter me, breath, his very oxygen. That if I sleep across enough, often, close, I will become what he's connected to.

Sometimes our union is strong, perfect, almost immortal. The boy I am under the lover cries out at this lot, that I will ever have to grow and leave this, his home.

Once I graduate from college, shortly thereafter.

I do not have an assured position in his life. I know my bond is tenuous, my tie.

It's different for his family. Parents mean the world to him. I'm less essential.

I was only a replacement originally for an empty spot left by the death of an actor he knew.

It was after the funeral that he came back to town and took me, decided to touch me, if that's what I wanted.

Then we do. I am dying for him, in a sense, abandoning childhood and entering it at the same time, a new one, everything over to him and his hands to learn over, start under, again with my idea of who I am.

I give him an invitation to my college graduation. He has other things on his mind, though. There's no time for a gift right now.

School ends. I'm out of college. Streets hold less purpose here. They don't hold me, for sure. My lover and I have settled into our cycle. He leaves, comes back. Leaves, back. Always, he could give me more but I always want more than ever.

And I want. Too much longing, want becomes longing, longing because not enough.

Longer before he's getting back the next time. I start turning over in the crowded bed that is his I'm making, crowding with my mere presence. Bed becomes his I'm in.

Sex becomes at least we are touching, at least he's looking at me now, there's nobody else.

I ask myself what I'm doing not getting up and going to school. I get so fixated I can't slow my mind down to the halt that is content.

He worries I'm not eating enough because I'm not earning enough. He can't always buy me dinner. It's not right. I should get a job, he thinks.

I look at myself and see how I'm starting to waste away, again. Just like when I first started school.

The end quickens when we slow down. Little every day problems he starts to have with me, my presence more and more near. We're so close, too close once he has to sit still long and sees that. I'm not going to go away.

And look at me. What am I doing here.

I'm in school, then I'm not. I know what to do with myself, then don't.

For graduation, his parents buy me a cactus. What I wanted. He told them I wanted a cactus.

Some friends of his would have come seen me march, if I had. But I didn't.

Now that I'm not going to school, I have to plan my future.

My mother sends a graduation card. Congratulations.

Good luck in the future, says my stepfather.

My mother, she wishes I had "love" and "happiness."

My stepfather, he signs his name.

We moved against each other, our rhythms echoed.

In and out of each other, like waves crashing, and hands clasping backs. He makes me short of breathe for different reasons. Always, that feeling of carrying around deep inside your lungs your past.

Schooling, after full years, almost four.

I beg him not to leave me once I finish school. I say I only need to figure things out. It makes perfect sense I'd be uneasy, that I'd feel confused once out of school. It has nothing to do with him. Everyone goes through it. It's only natural. I'll figure it out. Just bare with me.

I just don't know if we are living together or what. I just don't know if this is going to go any further, us, if we're living together or what. It's only going to take me some time to not need him so much. I've been so dependent on him, emotionally, physically so long.

I think we can work thorough the place I stand still in.

My mother buys invitations to announce my graduation, even though I won't walk in the ceremony.

Besides, it's only a technicality. Some formality.

I only want to let people know that I'm getting out, relatives I haven't talked to in ages. My mother thinks it's a good idea. There is a correct way to go about it, she explains.

She misses her children. She says her love for us grows every day.

2) Kansas

our lives are now entwined.

Patti Smith, "Land"

We still have a little time together before I set myself up, a request that he will reject. I need proof now that he does love me. I have gotten him to where now he sometimes says he does, when he's fucking me, or after, or sometimes even when he calls on the phone when away, even if he did say he thought love was stupid. He is being stupid with me. Doubt starts to crush me until it has to be proved I'm just imagining his excluding me from other areas of his life.

But he proves my fears founded. There are certain places he would never in a million years take me. I can't go to Kansas with him. I just asked. Opened mouth, set myself up.

He's already asked someone else, a friend of his.

I was hurt from that day forward, when he said no, when I asked him to let me be there with him.

I didn't want to hear about it later.

But he was smart enough, enough like he's always been shrewd enough to see I was a good time no longer. If he took me, he'd just have to think about how I would react in various situations that might come up. Would I behave? In the end, I'd just be too much stress. He wanted to enjoy himself.

We aren't going anywhere together. Because I won't set myself up to be let down again, not again, to be told no. Trust of myself in his hands lets up. No reason to tell him what I want, to confide in him like he always wanted me to. No reason to talk.

He comes back from that trip early for our anniversary. He at least does that much. I can at least talk to him, over dinner. Don't pout. Hasn't he taken the time to come back for our anniversary? He was at another celebration, came back to this dull town for me. Just to see me. Hasn't he proved that I mean something, that what we are is important to him?

He gives me my present, a gift he bought at the airport on his way back.

3) third year

For the next year three years, more, I will try to find my place in relation to him. How can I? And try to see what he sees in friends, any he'd rather be with than me.

No matter what I do, or how much love.

Our third anniversary.

Maybe I forget that he even tries, how hard he says he does, claims.

He didn't want to make a big deal out of that day and year, our third. Just like he didn't want to make a big deal out of our first or second, so we ended up having dinner with friends that night, visiting.

Throughout, I wait for him. Never feel like he's to stay.

I stay and wonder when he's going to leave.

The lover is going to London. Then California. He'll see his doctor while there. I can't tell anything, how he's feeling. The lover won't address. He says he's coming back. Then he doesn't.

He has to go somewhere else, first.

I'm hurt, I say.

He can't talk about that. Not now.

He has to go right now, his lunch date is at the door.

He hangs up the phone, at the hotel in California, where we once stayed.

a) the doctor

It's not like he can just take me in his arms, tell me everything is going to be all right, show me.

The doctor he turns to, believes completely in, doesn't want him touching me.

Because want articulated with my body is not answered, I close my mouth. I become even more silent.

He stops touching me, stops considering me.

He has to do what the doctor told him. The doctor knows how to make him well.

He was in a dental chair, his mouth being operated on. One of his teeth crumbled, causing him to go into a fetal convulsion. He regressed under the pain that far.

When we talk on the phone the next morning, he tells me how his dentist had to take him to a doctor. The dentist's brother, who could supposedly cure cancer and such, even AIDS patients. A Buddhist who would reroute my lover's energy. A rich Buddhist.

The Buddhist doctor brings up an earlier injury. Was there ever a loud popping sound between our bones when we were having sex? Us in bed. I'm my lover's main problem, the cause.

The enlightened man, Buddhist, and his wife who cooks dutifully then serves him as he consults with patients, doesn't understand. They've never met homosexuals before.

Then the doctor comes to visit, to stay with us. This man is going to make my lover better.

They set up camp, he and his entourage. They take days telling my lover what to make of his condition, how to go correct it. When he can touch me, and when it's best not to, how often he can. Weeks then months.

They aren't completely against me. They also prepare a couple of medicines for me, slowing down my questions of my lover, trying to help me be nice to him, never feel my place any longer.

They made a potion for us to drink before we had sex, when they said we could.

The potion makes my lover feel a complete union. He gets scared, because of this feeling. He wants to back off for awhile.

We've only got a few months to go, past the three year anniversary mark.

Then he can't touch me. Some doctor says so. He's not allowed, if he wants to get any better.

Touched, not. Caressed, barely hugged.

Not too long, too tight.

Not too much, long. Let go.

The doctor tells him what to do.

It is done subtly, swiftly, the way I'm uncovered as the root of his problems.

He will never wake from the way the doctor puts him to sleep to me.

I wake up so suddenly in the middle of the night.

It's too much. I am not small enough to be placed easily aside. This sobers. He doesn't like that, being sobered. He apologizes. He's sorry. He can't touch me anymore.

It could take over. He has to learn restraint. The doctor tells him to tell me no, if I really love him, I'll understand. My lover says even if he isn't touching me it means nothing. He still feels the same, he says. Nothing is that white and black.

Some doctor won't let me touch him.

One day he tells me to lock up the house behind me, when I leave.

Doubt has always been there. I was waiting for him to alleviate it, but then came when he no longer thought for himself. He has placed himself in the doctor's hands, the one who tells him everything he needs to do.

You have to trust completely, or it doesn't work.

b) car

My mother and her husband buy me a car one Christmas, toward the end of my relationship with the lover, after I graduate. It's used, so there'll have to be a title change.

And I have to get insurance. My mother goes into explaining it all. This is how you learn.

She has to have surgery, her gallbladder removed. She says you don't need it anyway.

It will take place through her bellybutton, the place where I was connected to her. In her wooden jewelry box, I remember the yellow plastic pin-clip with rings my sister and I try on when playing. My mother let us into her room playing dress up with her. All those special rings in a jewelry box and that yellow plastic clamp, the object that severed us, cut through our umbilical cord, line from mother daughter, mother to son.

Once he says he wishes he could just buy me a car because it would make some of my life so much easier.

But he can't, he can't do that.

Too much baggage goes along with that.

In the car, the clutch becomes a problem.

My lover takes me close for a driving lesson in my new car. Take it slowly around the neighborhood where I live. I want to stay here with him, don't go home for Christmas. I come up with all kinds of excuses. I don't want to have to return to where I came from. Want to drive, just get somewhere safe to look back from with him.

II.

A) Morning After, 3½ Yrs

It's just another day, the day we die.
In Spring, around April. After Valentine's day, before Easter.

He says later it was over long before that.
He says that it's been over for a long time, that he drug it out. And he apologizes for that. He's sorry, is always sorry later, after it's too late.
He stops the car to tell me, the sentence I've felt before coming. Felt him trying to find just the right words to put it in. He turns to me, at the most convenient time for him to tell me, says he's breaking us up.
Taking my hand in his.

One long scream. I am hysterical. Then another, at the top of my lungs forgotten in his car driving me home.

This is how he returns to me this time, to leave me. Some time the last time he went away he went for good. Became the deserter he is. Meeting me this time, this is just some common courtesy. He wouldn't be surprised if I never spoke to him again.

When he revokes our union, I'm in the middle of nowhere, his car.
There is nowhere for me to just open the door and walk off to. No way for me to leave him.
I scream, crying in his arms he takes me in.
His arms holding me, holding onto me, so I scream driving me back home as I pound against his back.

Then say nothing. Quit. Go quiet.

He drives me back to before the occasional limousine.

Past where I've been left.

He is stopping all this before we start hating each other, he says. Before we can no longer even bare the reality of the sight of each other, get a chance to hate each other. I don't know why that's the natural conclusion for him.

I get out of his car, let out, down. Go back to my house. Quit my crying.

Immediately the unbearable town shrinks even more constricting.

I won't stay here.

One day I wake up and go to the window. From my bed I see a procession of limos. One for each of the men he works with.

One big and white, but that's not his.

A black one, possibly.

More cars drive by.

I call him, because I need to know he is still there.

Still in that same hotel room I knew.

B) 3 Fs

1) fleeing

I asked him to change his mind. He wouldn't listen. There were other solutions, I begged. Begged of the lover, the one who said no. I have to get up, go, don't, don't touch him anymore. Stop trying to look him in the face, eyes. Meeting a hollow in my chest.

We need time apart. Maybe one day, he says.

The separation marks me deeper than the loss of my father because I am more aware.

Or becomes the same thing, because we are both older.

Or I am more left, because I beg him not to, show I care one way or the other.

Hurts the most, deepest, because I try to reason where there can be none. He won't let there be, his mind made up. I thought he was smarter than my father.

Once I cut my foot on something, a branch with thorns that rake it when we are on our way out to the pool, playing with the dogs in the big backyard.

The lover takes me inside, saying he has some salve, follow him and he'll apply thick medicine to a fresh wound.

Then lays me down on the vinyl couch, gets on top of me, makes love. One of the few times he ever does to me during day.

Saying he just wanted to get me inside, so he could.

Then we get back up, go back out into the bright day.

Once he decided we were too close for our own good, his, he started pulling away.

I felt, but there was nothing I could do.

He couldn't continue to place himself in the hands of someone he felt too aligned with, a perfect union with, too much.

Remember he said that.

He's so used to having me in his bed when he is here that I start to be part of going to bed for him. He is so used to having me beside him in that bed.

I have become part of the ill-state of his life, how he can't always keep going.

A reminder that he needs rest, of his emotion, worry, concern. Part of the sick bed.

From the bed we shared we go off into separate, new ones.

New beds. We move on.

Forward, in his words.

We have to move on, forward.

He will never need anyone like I have always needed someone.

He tells me he's not what I want. Once it becomes apparent I will never grow up, will always be too needy. He knows that, has figured that much out by now.

He says it was over a long time ago. It's been over for a long time, he drug it out. Too long, ever since he got back from Kansas where he didn't take me, wouldn't.

He apologizes for that, dragging it out, but not for excluding me.

Before I make up my mind to just go, let go, I make him acknowledge he might be making a mistake. He's at least thought of that.

It's possible.

But it's his mistake to make.

He kept asking what himself, what am I thinking? Look at him. What was he doing letting go of me, knowing he's not getting any younger.

He says of course he still has feelings for me. They've just been put in context, now.

But he still has feelings for me, after almost four years together.

I'm a friend like one of his other friends now.

No lover, trouble.

Not someone he has a lot to do with any longer.

Now we lock emotions inside.

I will have to start taking care of myself. I leave my windows open to street. I can't sleep. Our coming together ends.

From one of his friends, I hear he's getting back today. Isn't he coming back tonight? To town. Making everyone's lives exciting again by mere closeness. But I wouldn't know this.

For that first week or so, I can't eat.

For that first week or so, I am in denial, hanging onto his guilt, desire to make sure I'm not too wrecked before he takes leave again. I am trying to hang onto him by hanging onto that, any way I can.

I must decide whose side to take, his or my own, no longer being one and the same.

Nights, I'm not able to sleep when there isn't him to hold me. I keep telling myself I need no one.

I make tea, put on a record. It's raining against the open windows, nothing stopping it from coming in onto the floor collecting there.

I know life is changing again for the better, always for better.

I get a pair of shoes from him when he leaves me, and sheets. New sheets and shoes. He says he wants me to have nice things, clean sheets. He can't help it if he can provide for me and does.

If he feels like he's not what I need, we're not compatible, never were.

A year later, I'll still be wearing the shoes, even though the weather keeps them damp.

Still sleeping in those sheets, even though no longer clean.

Even when he leaves me, I still act like I want to be with him because I don't know what else to do. I can't just move away from him like I did the others. He's everywhere. My life becomes this pattern controlled by him.

I want to be close by, close enough to him so he can still reach me if he wants to.

Even if we can never go back to the beginning and fix this.

His face is everywhere, and his name. Written, spoken, print.

We're in rooms together in my mind, behind curtains a friend sewed for him, one who stays in town near when there's nothing here for us like him, family, friends.

We don't have the way he can just pick up and leave whenever he wants.

Back porch abandoned, plants in huge clay pots tended by gardener hired to do the job. Town becomes the place where we are left. He comes to visit, occasionally.

Friends and strangers talk about him, to me and among themselves. They talk. I overhear everything constantly. In passing, to my face. Passion of his name, what he's doing, occupying himself, what he's doing after that, everyone's lips.

What's he doing next?

Where he's going after that.

I will have to wait to see if he made the right decision for us. Wait to see if our lives really get better.

He isn't my lover anymore. He calls to leave messages, tell me he's home, how he's doing, what, ask me to page him, call him.

I can't kiss him. I have to let rooms separate us when I see him.

He fondles my hair.

He tries to come see me, to visit. He has work to do, has to go now. Work keeps us sane.

He says he's happy to hear my sister is having a baby. He's become just another man who can't understand.

Another man there's no point with.

He brings up history, says we have a lot of history together.

Plus, he has a present for me.

I take it, take anything because I'm passive.

My loving him was my lying there, believing he meant everything he said, still does, occasionally.

His only expression of affection now is purchasing. Buying me new clothes. He can afford to. My closet is full of ways I've looked near him. I can't possibly have it on my face to keep looking like this, keep dressing like his.

Nobody could be impartial enough.

At first, I'm not even supposed to tell anyone about us.

He said that way it would be easier. Just tell everyone we're good friends.

Then I feel like I can't trust anyone. Like I have no friends I can talk to about my life. I get another job, one I wear headphones at listening to a tape of songs over and over, a loop of new, not his, anything but his, those words he pens that give him means to enter greater worlds.

He's already left me, so I'm leaving the house with others. A girl who is my friend because we have things in common, used to live right next door to each other. I don't remember. She tells me. Remember her dog? How could I forget.

She asks me if I think I'll ever return to him.

There's been talk of it, but this could be just how he eases the shock of finality. Could be false hope.

I don't tell her, though. I comfort in maybe, in ten years or so, he said.

The girl I'm with says he and I will be so handsome then, men only get better looking with age.

I picture him in that yard we spent early afternoons in when he was here, when I was. I see him walking over alone those grounds of his.

Someone will come visit him.

He will fill up his houses, all of them, with the spoils of his travels. He will bring the world around him, to him, gather it in manageable clumps, objects that can be set down, forgotten, not protest to be taken out and held again.

Objects that will sit there until he sees them again.

He will age with his family. They will grow old together, keep aging, steering, trusting.

He will have to keep making decisions. Right or wrong, he will find a way to stand by them. Must. That's the way his mind works.

He stays overseas longer and longer, in hotel rooms he can easily afford.

On the sets of the movies he is instrumental in. He starts calling less and less, talking less about anything, more about nothing.

His houses wait at home. I realize it's an illusion he ever went anywhere at all with me.

After graduation, he leaves me. I am trying to find somewhere new to live. There are a couple of letters from him, and postcards, attempts at maintaining contact he controls and feels safe with.

The first letter comes from the set of a film, written in his touching script, not typed, hotel letterhead. He tells me how the movie he's watching be made is going, well. Also how happy he wants me to be. It's a long letter for a man like him with so many people to see. Forget I would have never gotten anything like this if he was still with me. He tells me how well he's sleeping, about his health, fit he's feeling, how much I mean to him, all his love.

He only writes letters after he leaves me, more than I can say for my father.

It's only because of him that I ever graduate from college at all. He gave me dedication to hold myself down and in place, convince myself I was working towards something important.

I get enough from him to sit there in class, let life lull for those hours.

His influence on me is greater than anything I learn in my books anyway, will always be. He's what this world values, I know.

I haven't yet seen the film he went away to produce. Stayed away so long making I got so lonely. Plus, he'd stopped touching me.

In the film, a boy has a part where you know he loves another boy or a man. I'm still unclear on how age factors in.

The film touches him. But he sees my feelings in no reel.

He explains what the word "dailies" means, like I don't know.

I wear my hair like the boys in the film. He likes my hair when I wear it that way, holding onto trying to tame it for him.

Every night before I got to sleep I imagine where he is away. My hair fans out on the pillow, curling under length, locks, just reaching past my shoulders.

He took gobs of it in his hand, doesn't want me to cut it because one day I'll regret it, he says. When I no longer have it, just look at him.

I have nothing else to pull from my eyes.

I'm still part of the town. It's there I work to the disregard of my desires. It's in the small circles, low expectations of people, pettiness of the artists, the lack of motion. Fullness of my nap, dawning of my dreams, I know I could be someone somewhere else.

The streets are longer and longer and no longer connect. Others will occupy him. For a while, or maybe longer. I don't know which possibility hurts more, will hurt me more.

Here, I no longer have a destination.

When I had him I didn't worry about myself. I was something, or I was his.

He was satisfied by my looks or way I touched him, what I gave. Must have been. He wouldn't have kept me so long, touching. Unless he had come to value my friendship. But I never wanted to be his friend, like all those friends I've met.

One day, though, that's the option I'm left with.

I must grow calm, settle, settle for something else, forget this part.

Turn to the moon again, on certain nights.

I want to be trusting again. It doesn't matter. It's not my world. It doesn't matter what I think I've felt. A wedding imagined falls apart.

A substantial affair lands on the floor.

I'm looking to breathe, mouth to his mouth. My only past reason. I kiss pictures, pictures of the lover. I look for new pictures to kiss. I don't think I can keep repeating this. Over and over.

His body is a piece of paper.

I knew my days were numbered. I saw him packing, saw him never coming back. I saw myself in my rented room filled with boxes, lack of ever having laid everything out in front of me.

My mother wants to know what I'm going to do. I don't know, move somewhere, find another lover.

There has to be some way to cover up this left hole.

It's one of the bars in our town.

Once it was the most popular. That night, like many nights, I couldn't sleep for want of him.

That's what starts it all over. As soon as I see there is no one left, I go looking for someone to replace what I've lost. I wait. I wait for the bartender to finish night's work. I wait longer and longer for the waiting to stop.

And then the boy walks through the door with casual invitations and lips thick with pouts for me. I look up. He is a very tall man, with boy eyes. A southern boy, as well. I recognize my hatred was masked love, the lack of his presence. The boy is just like my lover only less successful, so much closer to me than anywhere near that ideal. We are walking together in the night becoming morning. We could go to his house or mine. We've eaten where I once worked, before I quit after the first night of the lover. Didn't I want to?

He socializes in a trust of other boys I've never known.

My hurt is so deep I want to fall into hold. Must be dumb, resigned to hurt.

My fear is I've had the only love I could ever and lost it. Control of my life. I've shown I cared, tried not to care, acted like I didn't. Acted so well even I believed and bought it. Acted so long I've forgotten how to wake up and recover.

Maybe some of his friends will side with me. When they can drop their faces and close eyes, must admit to themselves how hard it must be. I was so young. I started out so impressionable, a boy at the beginning of his education, feeling emotion run its course, trying to make him into something he never was.

So in the wake of me, us, the lover has a small price to pay. Always so much outside of me.

I proceed with timid steps.

Over dinner, we are quiet. Quiet after the fact.

All I want to do is put my head in the lap of the man who used to be my lover.

He concedes. After dinner, on a porch swing.

The lover has to get back to work now. I have nowhere to go. That's why I don't want to go yet. He says we will be closer this way, able to be more intimate without sex, not further apart.

Plus, if I move to the city, he goes all the time, so we will both be there, in the city together. On occasion.

For a year he tries to put a safe distance between us. So later I owe him even more, my freedom.

Further distrust of most things male.

He wants me to have clean sheets. He buys them for me.

He calls from a hotel room, one of the many, says imagine, I know exactly where he is.

In a hotel. In that bed with him I've been. I know the one, know the way hall leads to the living room. From the bedroom, view of the city from the balcony, white gauze curtains billow as caught by breeze. White pillows, kitchen.

The picture behind the bed, on the wall.

A general, in all his finery. War-paint, fatigues.

I go off to New York, a brief trip.

Thought I might live there.

I walk trying to convince myself I have a stable grasp on what can only be perceived as slipping away from him.

I've never touched Brian C. Brian C. is in New York, slouched over a book, at a table.

I recognize his neck, call out, words, air up against him. We happen to be in the same restaurant, where the world stops. I tell him I'm going to move there. He lives and works in New York. He asks me about my high school boyfriend, B. Haven't talked to him in forever. We don't keep in touch.

Brian looks exactly the same. He was in a fashion spread in this month's *SPIN*. He's a model. I find out from someone else he lives with his boyfriend. He never talks about that. Not to me. My fascination must unsettle him.

He says he saw my picture in *Blindspot*.

I don't know how many men come in he waits on, slides his phone number. Brian C. But he doesn't make moves towards me, doesn't see past the boy I was in school, those days I silently gawked, fumbling with my own zipper, the boy with all the vicarious connections now. No matter how far I move, I'll always be moving up behind him.

I see Brian C. as the only worthwhile aspect of that place I'm emerging from, my only fidelity to a past before the lover. The only body deserving any veneration.

I go to Providence, Rhode Island. I eat away months of life. Go back to the town. Go to Memphis, then somewhere in North Carolina. Go to Virginia, then back. To San Francisco, then back to the town. I plan to go away again.

Plan to go back to New York, to Paris, to become untraceable, different from him.

I will flee, by myself or with a friend. These days, periods between any state where I feel living, is recovery of my stillness, my thought process.

The arid state of waiting for the next stirring of something.

I've been here for almost six years. Out of school nearly two.
Walking down the street I see him.
But these days he's here even less, less and less.
As he moves further away from who it was I felt.

He got an apartment in New York, broke down and did it. It has a lot to do with the whole movie business.

He lets me stay in one of his buildings in the town where I'm still trying to live, for the time being. Because he is rich, and worries about me, even though we're no longer together. And it's easy for him to try and want to take care of me. Even though I am technically no longer his concern.

Except for the apartment, I have no reason to stay.

I don't pay rent, but that's because the place is being renovated as I'm trying to live there. Things get covered with dust.

I see the street, draw a map that connects all the places I've lived, when with him, when without. I moved so many times.

I wanted to leave after he left me, immediately. Pack bags and go. No reason to stay here, out of school.

But I told him I'd stay if he gave me a place. Agreed to that. Landlord I could trust, if he'd become at least that.

He agreed only until I got back on my feet. I didn't know when that would be.

The duplex where I took him in. The first time. I felt I could do anything there, be anything. Starting new, over, fresh.

Felt like I could stay forever, that I was starting my own life. My first home as an adult.

One day he drops me off. We were going to meet later for dinner, later if not, after he'd gone and had a drink.

He would be ready for me to come over. Then we could sleep together.

The landlord had been trying to reach me, but I hadn't been around. I had to move. He was selling the house.

Gone would be the place where all my memories has been housed so far.

I always knew I would have to move someday. The boxes stayed where they were.

The house I move into, one of many he owns all over town, is still being worked on. The men are there outside during the day. They come in to work around me, other days. Nailing, painting some wall, redoing roof, digging holes in yard to place new pipes.

Nights they go home and I sleep with myself, as cars, voices and lights of engines speeding-up, driving pass and then past.

I say when trying to tell stories to others who don't know me that well, "This guy that I was involved with for four years."

Not who he is.

As part of the renovation going on in the house, the gas heaters are removed.

There will be central heat now, no use cleaning up. I will be leaving soon. Soon it will be painted all again.

Ready, fixed up. Brought to a state I could live in, I will be asked to move.

Clean sheets we parted with, all the nice clothes, new shoes, covered in soot left by some past burning, holes knocked into ceiling that blacken everything I have I haven't given away yet.

Summer, when we should be relaxing, splashing in pools.

Summer, I lie in bed, a rented room.

I take shoes off and turn on radio, for any noise to distract me from beating my heart.

I read before bed, knowing he isn't coming to disturb me.

What's done is done.

His car goes down a different street, drives a different way so he doesn't pass light in the window, signal I'm still inside.

He wonders why I can't get on with my life.

I try to find anything to look at to not have to look at how I live, how alone, my mother right.

I will die a lonely old man, that threat she used to try to scare me out of acting like who she saw me turning into, becoming more and more when still young.

It is a few months or more before my final departing from his town, during the afternoon, the weather already too hot to function very effectively. Friends visit him. I stop turning to my mother, not like she could understand. Then, in a sudden dawning, I no longer have a home. There I am walking through my life but not feeling it and waking up to walk through it and no longer wanting to live it at all.

I start to feel my age, between everything, beyond everything, marked and ruined already. Running in place. This is the part where no one can help me, no one can reach me, no one can go along with me.

People keep meeting. People keep believing they are living. Or else this is good enough for them, more than enough, this life.

Silence of years will prevail and become the basis, standard.

The trembling of bodies in dreams, only.

And in dreams are all hopes, obstacles scattered.

He will forgive my trespasses, ask maybe about mother, as he thinks of his. May ask about the child my sister will bear.

Small talk will give way to only breath that issues from open holes, nostrils, mouth. Between fingers.

Lips press against lips, nose angles in cross below, to side of another, in a doorway, entrance.

Let me in.

Maybe we will feel we still love each other. He finally said so one morning when coming out of sleep together, just there beside each, pillows. My head a little below his, adoring, on his shoulder, looking up whispering.

When he was at home on my back.

2) family

a) my mother

My mother helps me buy plane tickets, once he no longer flies me any closer. She calls periodically.

She just wanted to tell me how my sister is somewhere also upset.

My mother wants to know if we're still friends, me and the man who was my lover. He still calls.

She really liked him.

My mother sends me long letters at first, then short notes.

Their whole world, my mother and her husband, is their yard, house, and jobs. My only family for miles. Sometimes they go to the lake.

My mother goes to the cold to visit her mother. Or in the summer, to Florida where my grandparents have a second house.

It takes an effort to keep two people together. My mother asks me to be her Valentine. She goes shopping for me, buying a card in a store.

Decal decorations, gold papers, little 50s left over my grandparents anniversary celebration swim in front of my eyes. "Love" and "Happiness" are underlined, scored twice. That's all my mother wants for me. She tells me to tell him she said hello.

Golden decals for 50 years fill envelopes. How long my grandparents have been married, almost forever. By now, more than that. They will always be married, forever.

Grandparents on my mother's side, the only ones I know.

They were married in June, during the summer. My grandmother never goes back to school.

I'm sent two tickets to their celebration ceremony, golden anniversary. I don't go, can't bring myself.

My mother sends me a napkin, souvenir from the service. I don't know what to do with a piece of paper. I have no book to put it in, no souvenir file.

I keep it in a drawer for awhile like important documents. It doesn't seem right to just throw it away.

Since neither my sister or I were there, absent grandchildren, the family sat pictures of us on a table covered in white paper, a long banquet. This way people can see we do exist. My graduation picture next to my sister in military uniform. One day I throw away the napkin.

A card with a bird on it, she sends me when she still sends money, back when I was in school. The cards are all in a shoe box, now.

She tries to persuade me to get insurance, now that I am no longer in school and can no longer cover me. What if I have to go into the hospital again, ever? She knows I don't want to think about this, but should. What if I lose my house? She wants to help me come up with a plan.

She misses her children. We are no children, never were.

She sends a card, underlining "unique" and "special." I no longer believe anything.

There's a single gold star on the card cover, like in second grade or so for good work.

Back when I still wanted some girl in my class to say I was her doll baby's father, let me be that.

There are other cards, a whole garden of flowers kept in a drawer of my desk.

An assortment of roses, and a smiling face of some boy that's not me.

Here, away from my mother, I turned 19 through 24.

i)
She says she gives me what she can. Ten dollars.

I'm not eating, not well.

I pay to get tested to try to get into another school, higher.

ii)
I've called Florida where they are all visiting. Grandparents want to see me, no longer feel like they know me.

My mother wants me to call her.

iii)
Do I have my grandparents' phone number?

My stepfather isn't going this time to Florida. Just my mother and sister. My mother will hug my sister for me.

iv)
Bill collectors are looking for me. And a landlord whose lease I

broke. They are trying to find me through my parents, like they're still responsible for me.

v)

Another check bounces.

My mother wants my last lover's address so she can send him a Christmas card.

vi)

Their lucky thirteenth anniversary, my mother and my stepfather. She sends a picture of herself in a bathing suit, showing the scale, height, how tall the sunflowers in her backyard have grown. Giant beanstalks. Another picture of their swimming pool, above ground variety, and the wooden deck my stepfather built around.

In another, she looks surprised in the embrace of my sister's husband. My sister who manages to marry, snag a man. Almost four years now.

b) sister

My sister's wedding announcement. Plain ivory cream paper folded
four times.
   In half, and then again. Almost a perfect square.
   No writing on the front, words at all.
   Only imprint, press of roses, roses defining a border. Plot,
picture frame.
   Roses inside a picture frame.
   Roses the color of the paper, white.
   January.
   Where do they go? England. Or back South.
   All I know is they marry at city hall, ten o'clock.
   Who is their witness? How long do they kiss?
   Nobody knows.

Before England for my sister, there is Texas. That's where she starts
her military job, training takes place. She joins, and that's where she
must have married. She met her husband in boot camp.
   She wanted to tell me what married life is like, so she picks out a
card. She thinks this says it all, a kid's crayon drawing on the front
in wax-colors.
   Sun orange-yellow-red, smiling with a red upturned line.
   The house blue with eyes for windows, and a purple roof, red
door.
   Two flowers easy to make in a child's hand. One yellow coward,
other orange-rust.
   Sky blue, clouds white, light gray.
   Sun's eyes purple, grass green.

My sister gets married, gets a TV.

I only see television in hotel rooms, when traveling. My lover didn't have one in his house, either.

He kept it in his cabin, that first place he took me.

My sister is going to have a child. Once her husband gets back home from where he was stationed, after Christmas. She will reward him when he comes back with the baby he's always wanted. It's the least she can do, her present to him. Plus, they've not been getting along so well, lately, so maybe this will help. It's time. They've been married almost three years already.

It helps my sister if she can hold up my mother and our stepfather as an example.

Remember they fought. That helps, she says. They fought all the time. And they're still married. She's only normal. It's only natural she and her husband yell constantly, wake the baby to screaming back and forth, hurling elementary insults.

The sound the baby wakes to in the crib, permanent disagreement.

She guesses she shocked the extended family, getting married so young. The first grandchild married. And the first to bear a great-grandchild, on both sides of the family, my mother and my stepfather's. We wouldn't know about our father's.

I don't know who knows what, haven't seen the extended family. Don't really ask our mother about them. Don't know what they know about me, either.

My sister is in London. New job, husband. She sends me a letter about when she came down to visit and have a dinner with our mother and my lover and his family. She took a picture of my lover's nephew, my lover holding him.

My sister is afraid she overstepped her boundaries by taking the picture without asking. Says he can have all copies of any picture he's in. Sends all the pictures back for me to give to him, afraid to keep any memories of that dinner.

3) fin, 3 fotos

a) another picture of him

I find a picture of him in a magazine a friend is throwing away. He's caught at a concert, another place I never went. Aging, you can tell, but he looks happy, pleased with himself. He's getting better, so much better without me. Doesn't take much to make him happy. He always said, was always reminding. Yet at some point, I ceased doing the trick.

He's being watched, so he knows he exists.

I often came to doubt this of myself. Especially now, without him. What did we used to mean to each other? I forget.

He likes that it doesn't matter, not this split between us, this rift. Ever did. He's gone on. He's older, wiser. Enlightened, and learned so much more. He has something to say now about all this success in his life. Voice and public, a sounding board.

Life that does not sink back to from where it came, corner crawled back into, curled up when it seems like all you will ever know is all you ever did.

If I was caught in a moment, any, I don't think I would ever come across like him.

b) us, on beach

The one who killed herself took the only picture I have with me of my lover and I together. She worked in his office. We were all going to a wedding. I was a bus boy at the time, but his boyfriend. I went, as did the men he works with and their wives or girlfriends. The only family was family of the bride and groom.

We were there on that beach, in Florida, a weekend.

How we were together those nights in that hotel are some of my most vivid memories. Defy dying.

Jacksonville, Florida. We have a terrace that opens out to the sea.

On that beach we walk along, side by side, our hands even brush on occasion. We are caught enjoying the sun together. His straw hat on and tan shorts to swim in, hair on chest fine black mist. I carry a red beach bag, full of our gear. My denim shorts, blond hair still long, and curly, curling.

We are almost arm in arm. At night the wedding celebration spills over everywhere. We go back to our room after the pool, the hot tub, the ocean, in the dark together. He slides over and into me. He is more sober than at home. Thus more attentive. He is biting my ear lobe, whispering wants, requests, into the hole above it, thrusting into me. I let him fuck me two nights in a row, two spent in that hotel. Even though no condoms. He looked for them, didn't find any. Even though the first time I wanted him bare, he said he'd never fuck without a condom. Ever.

Now he has. There.

We wear almost matching suits. We have a wedding to go to. It's the first I've ever been to. The woman who works for him, not the one getting married and out of the office, but the one who took our picture on the beach is there. Not getting married. She thought she was, before she killed herself.

After Christmas she does it. She was going to get married. Then she went to New York, to visit his or her family. Something happened. She was found back in town in her apartment, her closet.

I was with a wife of one of his associates when the call came. Just like the old days. Immediately I wanted to be at his side, to help him through.

He wanted to be there for me.

I thought this death might change everything. Like the earlier one we were built on, the boy I never knew, the one after that, when I was with him. Plus now.

c) picture

In a photograph in his house, we are nearing our second Christmas. I'm wearing a shirt he bought me. We are on the side of a stage in Atlanta. His arm around me, my shoulder. I'm standing there, letting him, holding myself like I can't believe in the lasting of this snapped moment. Knowing it's going away, the way I'm not grinning, hurry up and take it.

By the way he's almost picking me up, knocking me over, pleased as punch, tilting me I can see he's proud of me. Holding me, his arm around me.

The way I'm reluctant to pose, I see I already feel too aware, out of place, don't belong, or any observer could pick up on that. Project that onto me. I see the way I feel unkempt, too much of my own to slip into any setting. Am starting to doubt if I can go anywhere with him, falling out from under that grip.

Feel less entwined. It's just one picture. Could just be a particularly rough period, but at least we were together.

Even if he was letting us as a pair be captured in a moment forever, I feel deeper I am being hidden. Because not everyone he knew had to draw some conclusion about my place.

But here I am, in this one picture.

We weren't really dating. It's was more than that the moment it commenced.

I can never see certain people again in the same light, feel the same privileged place I once occupied in his arms. Where there have been others like me he left.

The texture of his shirt has become my grounding, is grounding.

I can feel him in my hands, even though we will never be seen as fertile together.

Athens, GA February—May 1998
Brooklyn, NY January—June 1999

Born in Virginia and raised in Georgia, **DOUGLAS A. MARTIN** moved to New York at 25 and now resides in Brooklyn. Douglas's writing spans fiction and nonfiction, traversing poetry and prose with works translated into Italian, Japanese, and Portuguese. Past books include: *Once You Go Back* (Lambda Award nomination in the Gay Memoir/Biography category), *Branwell* (Ferro-Grumley Award finalist), several volumes of poetry, and a book of stories. *Outline of My Lover* was named an International Book of the Year in The Times Literary Supplement and adapted in part by the Forsythe Company for their ballet and live film "Kammer/Kammer." Publications with Nightboat Books include a book-length essay and lyric study, *Acker*, a prose triptych, *Your Body Figured*, and most recently a novel, *Wolf*.

HUGH RYAN is writer, curator, and public historian in New York City. He is the author of *When Brooklyn Was Queer*.

Nightboat Books

Nightboat Books, a nonprofit organization, seeks to develop audiences for writers whose work resists convention and transcends boundaries. We publish books rich with poignancy, intelligence, and risk. Please visit nightboat.org to learn about our titles and how you can support our future publications.

The following individuals have supported the publication of this book. We thank them for their generosity and commitment to the mission of Nightboat Books:

Kazim Ali
Anonymous
Jean C. Ballantyne
Photios Giovanis
Amanda Greenberger
Elizabeth Motika
Benjamin Taylor
Peter Waldor
Jerrie Whitfield & Richard Motika

In addition, this book has been made possible, in part, by grants from the New York City Department of Cultural Affairs in partnership with the City Council and the New York State Council on the Arts Literature Program.